THE STORIES OF F. SCOTT FITZGERALD
Volume 3: The Pat Hobby Stories

In Scott Fitzgerald, as in every writer of genius, there was something of the seer. He gave a name to an age – the Jazz Age – lived
through that age, and saw it burn itself out. As a *New York Times*
editorial stated after his death: 'He was better than he knew, for in
fact and in the literary sense he invented a "generation" . . . he
might have interpreted them and even guided them, as in their
middle years they saw a different and nobler freedom threatened
with destruction.'

F. Scott Fitzgerald was born in St Paul, Minnesota, and even as a
schoolboy in St Paul he was writing, and later at Princeton. In
1917 he left Princeton for the army – but didn't get to France –
and wrote in his spare moments. Then came *This Side of Paradise* –
the first of his novels – followed by two volumes of short stories,
and at last *The Great Gatsby*, which alone would assure Scott
Fitzgerald's place among writers of major stature. He died in
1941.

Besides *The Great Gatsby* and *This Side of Paradise*, he wrote three
other novels, *The Beautiful and the Damned*, *Tender is the Night*, and
The Last Tycoon (his last and unfinished work): four volumes of
short stories; and *The Crack-Up*, a selection of his autobiographi-
cal pieces.

All his works have been published in Pen

The Stories of F. Scott Fitzgerald

Volume 3

The Pat Hobby Stories

With an introduction
by Arnold Gingrich

Penguin Books

PENGUIN BOOKS

Published by the Penguin Group
Penguin Books Ltd, 27 Wrights Lane, London W8 5TZ, England
Penguin Books USA Inc., 375 Hudson Street, New York, New York 10014, USA
Penguin Books Australia Ltd, Ringwood, Victoria, Australia
Penguin Books Canada Ltd, 10 Alcorn Avenue, Toronto, Ontario, Canada M4V 3B2
Penguin Books (NZ) Ltd, 182–190 Wairau Road, Auckland 10, New Zealand

Penguin Books Ltd, Registered Offices: Harmondsworth, Middlesex, England

First published in the USA 1962
Published in Penguin Books in Great Britain 1967
10 9

Printed in England by Clays Ltd, St Ives plc
Set in Linotype Pilgrim

Contents

Introduction by Arnold Gingrich   7

Pat Hobby's Christmas Wish   25

A Man in the Way   36

'Boil Some Water – Lots of It'   43

Teamed with Genius   51

Pat Hobby and Orson Welles   62

Pat Hobby's Secret   72

Pat Hobby, Putative Father   80

The Homes of the Stars   89

Pat Hobby Does His Bit   98

Pat Hobby's Preview   108

No Harm Trying   117

A Patriotic Short   128

On the Trail of Pat Hobby   134

Fun in an Artist's Studio   139

Two Old-Timers   147

Mightier Than the Sword   153

Pat Hobby's College Days   160

Appendix   169

Introduction

This book's seventeen stories, comprising the entire Pat Hobby sequence, bridge the last major gap in the collected writings of F. Scott Fitzgerald.

But this volume is more than a collection of previously uncollected short stories. For while its several episodes were originally published as a series of separate sketches, Fitzgerald began thinking of them, after the first three were written, as a collective entity. Almost every time he wrote another, he would reconsider the order of their appearance in print and as long as he lived he kept revising them, just before their publication. Some were revised up to four times. The revisions were in some instances caused by considerations of the interdependence of the various parts in constituting the over-all delineation of the character of Pat Hobby.

Thus, while it would be unfair to try to judge this book as a novel, it would be less than fair to consider it as anything but a full-length portrait. It was as such that Fitzgerald worked on it, and would have wanted it presented in book form, after its original magazine publication. He thought of it as a comedy.

At the time of his death in December 1940, two thirds of the way through its publication, we referred to the Pat Hobby sequence as his 'last word from his last home, for much of what he felt about Hollywood and about himself permeated these stories'.

The continuity of the original publication was unbroken,

beginning in January 1940 and continuing without interruption for seventeen months, through May 1941.

Fitzgerald's literary stock was at its all-time low, and the obituary notices, almost without exception, gave no hint that this 'forgotten' author of the Twenties might ever be read again. Except for the then current Pat Hobby stories, none of his work was any longer in the public eye. Typical of the appraisals at the moment of his passing, and by no means the least kind, was this, in the *Chicago Daily News*:

When he died at 44, F. Scott Fitzgerald, hailed in 1922 as the protagonist and exponent of the Flapper Age, was almost as remote from contemporary interest as the authors of the blue-chip stock certificates of 1929. He was still writing good copy, but no one was mistaking a story writer for the Herald of an Era.

As soon as we could answer that (in the pages of the March '41 issue of *Esquire*, the one magazine that had never been closed to him), we reminded the *Chicago Daily News* that in literature there is no more insecure grip on immortality than that of a Herald of an Era, while a story writer may very well live forever. Twenty-one years is only a short step toward eternity, yet here now, over twenty-one years later, is the good copy that story writer was writing at that time.

But that his own expectations, at that moment, squared more nearly with those of the American press, who dismissed him as if he were a sort of verbal counterpart of John Held, Jr, was evident in his last letter to our office, a matter of days before his death, in which he spoke of the unfinished novel that was to be published posthumously (*The Last Tycoon*) as 'a book I confidently expect to sell all of a thousand copies'.

In the beginning, he didn't give the Pat Hobby project

even that much of a sendoff. The first Pat Hobby story came in on September 16, 1939, from what Scott called his hide-out address, 5521 Amestoy Avenue, Encino, California. Just above the address he had written in pencil, 'Hide-out address! Now that I've paid off 99/100 of my debts people want me to contract more.' He was working on the Universal lot at the time, was not drinking, thanks to Sheilah Graham's watchful care, and after having been ill for four months earlier in the year, was in a happy and productive working streak. He had sent in three stories that we had accepted in the previous six weeks ('Design in Plaster', 'Lost Decade', and 'Between Planes') and a fourth, about a father and his son, that hadn't quite jelled. He took that one back, to try to fix it, and then sent in the first Pat Hobby story, 'A Man in the Way', with the following note:

I have tried twice to fix the father-and-son story but there is something wrong structurally. I shall try it again next Sunday.

Meanwhile, perhaps this will take its place. If so, will you kindly wire me as usual. I can't calm down after a story till I know if it's good or bad.

Weekends were reserved for stories, since Universal took up his weekdays, and the next one, instead of being devoted to further tinkering on the story with which there was something wrong structurally, resulted in another tale about Pat Hobby 'who used to be a good man for structure'. Here is the note that came with it, on September 21, 1939:

Here's another story about Pat Hobby, the scenario hack, to whom I am getting rather attached. Also some enclosed pages with corrections for the first story about him ('Man in the Way').

Once again can I get a Western Union acceptance – that is if you like it wire me and wire the money to the Bank of America, Culver City.

I think I'll do one more story about this character Saturday or Sunday. In that case – and if you like it – that will give you six of my things. I wish to God you could pay more money. These have all been stories, not sketches or articles and only unfit for the big time because of their length.

Added poignancy is now lent to the above plea by the realization that the term 'sketches' was the one Scott always used to refer to such things as the now-famous Crack-up series of 1936. 'The Crack-Up', 'Pasting It Together', and 'Handle With Care'. (A couple of years before he had passed out saying 'Read those sketches to Sheilah, while I take a nap.')

Six days later, on September 27, 1939, came the following:

Here are some improvements for the second Hobby story, 'Boil Some Water'.

And on October 2, 1939, came the third, 'Teamed With Genius':

Once again the address is the Bank of America, Culver City, and I wish you'd wire the money if you like this story. Notice that this is pretty near twenty-eight hundred words long. I'd like to do some more of these if your price made it possible.

Would you wire me too, what you think of it?

That letter was followed by this wire, two days later:

Am sending revised version of last story stop don't set it up until it comes regards

And two days after that, October 6, 1939, two revised scripts came in with this note:

Enclosed is a copy of 'Teamed With Genius' revised. Do you think the Pat stories would be effective if published in one issue, or would that be against your budget system? I mean it would only be worth doing as a feature.

The following sounds crazy but I picked up the second Pat

Hobby story and liked it so well that I thought I'd make that one a little better also. I hope it's not too late to use this version.

Enclosed were the second version of the third story, and the third version of the second story.

On October 14, 1939, the fourth and fifth stories came in together.

With the fourth, 'Pat Hobby's Christmas Wish': 'Here's another Pat Hobby story. Again will your usual emolument to me be telegraphic?'

With the fifth, 'Pat Hobby's Preview': 'Again the old ache of money. Again will you wire me, if you like it. Again will you wire the money to my Maginot Line: The Bank of America, Culver City.'

Two days later, October 16, 1939, came this wire:

This request should have been inclosed with Pat Hobby's Christmas Wish which is three thousand words long if you can't go up by $150 I will have to send it East I hate to switch this series but can't afford to lose so much please wire me.

Answer:

Sending $150 today which will credit against purchase of Pat Hobby's Christmas Wish if you insist since that one has been rushed through for January issue and I can't do otherwise. However if you insist upon this arrangement for this story will have to decline with regret any more in this series. Would have been pleased to go on stocking them up against future requirements as fast as you could turn them out but cannot do so any more unless and until you let me be the judge of how much we can honestly afford to pay for them. Realize you haven't asked for my advice but would nevertheless advise you frankly not to jeopardize old reliable instant payment market like this by use of strong arm methods which I am bound to resent as reflection on my six year record of complete frankness in dealing with you. In any case you have the extra $150 and next move is up to you but on bird in hand theory believe you would be better businessman to regard it as advance against another story. Regards.

Imagine calling Scott a 'businessman', even in the heat of a hot wire. But two hours later he was calling me much worse, long distance collect. Miraculously, the connexion wasn't cut, though on other occasions it had been, when his rage had towered above the limits of language permitted by the telephone company, so it is only memory which seems to censor what he must have said to provoke this second wire of that day:

Dear Scott: We Mennonites cool down quicker than you fighting Irish so suggest you don't answer this until tomorrow but after you hung up I realized that if my unfortunate choice of words in my wire hurt you half as much as your last spoken words hurt me then it is ineffably silly for two adults to fight a mutually unwanted war over a relatively small amount of money. Upon re-reading our two wires I now frankly confess that yours did not warrant my use of the phrase 'strong arm methods' for which I apologize and can only ask you to forgive and forget. Meanwhile I assure you that our corporate troops may always be counted upon as allies to be summoned at will to your bread and butter Maginot Line. And I deeply regret that my ill temper should have burst so utterly without provocation and spattered such a sensitive soul as your good sweet self. Excuse it please.

Well, he must have, for I can neither remember nor find any answer to that, but my next wire read 'Appreciate the good word', and the next story came in, on October 27, 1939, with this note

Pay for this what you like. It's not up to the last story – yet it belongs to the series.

At the same time I wish you'd drop me a general opinion about whether you think Pat has run his course or not.

You'll telegraph, won't you?

So I did, as follows: 'Hobby title No Harm Trying is very good in the series and perhaps only seems below par to you because you are tiring of him, but please don't. He's good for consecutive series of twelve at least and will make you a nice book afterwards. Wiring money. Regards.'

On November 8, 1939, came 'Pat Hobby's College Days', with this note:

On your advice I am going on with the Hobby series for at least two more. This is an in and outer, but I think certainly as good as the last.

Thanks, by the way, for your very concrete opinion about the series in general. It was most encouraging.

The usual wire to hold for corrected copy followed, and on November 13, 1939, came another story, 'Pat Hobby's Young Visitor', followed almost immediately by the expected wire to hold that one, too, for a corrected version.

Then, in December, after two telegraphed requests for wired reinforcements to the Maginot Line at Culver City, came another story on the nineteenth, 'Two Old Timers', with a note explaining that he'd 'been sick in bed again and gotten way behind'.

By this time, the first of the stories to appear in print, 'Pat Hobby's Christmas Wish', had come out in our issue dated January, 1940, eliciting this comment from Scott:

I felt in spite of the title being appropriate to the season it was rather too bad to begin the Pat Hobby series with that story because it characterizes him in a rather less sympathetic way than most of the others. Of course, he's a complete rat but it seems to make him a little sinister which he essentially is not. Do you intend to use the other stories in approximately the order in which they were written?

Thus began the endless shuffling of the order of appearance of the various stories, on which he seemed to have new thoughts every time another in the series was delivered.

This, together with keeping track of the first, second and third drafts, and charging off the right advances against the right stories, and coping with the telegrams that began asking why he hadn't heard anything about a given story, that often preceded its receipt in the mails, made the editing of the Pat Hobby series an overtime job. Production took no notice of holidays, as witness this wire, filed after office hours on December 22, 1939:

that you wire a hundred advance on really excellent story to reach you Tuesday so I can buy turkey is present Christmas wish of

'Pat Hobby Fitzgerald'

The money was wired that night, and on Christmas Day, 1939, he mailed the story, 'Mightier Than the Sword', with this note:

Please wire money. Thanks. Did you know that last story (Two Old Timers) was the way 'The Big Parade' was really made? King Vidor pushed John Gilbert in a hole – believe it or not.

'Your chattel'

The next, 'A Patriotic Short', was mailed on January 8, and followed four days later by a wire asking whether I got it, to which my secretary unguardedly answered that I was out of town, which brought her a wire telling her, as if she of all people didn't know, that 'my arrangement with Mr Gingrich has been always based on payments upon delivery for his series stop must realize on this story somewhere by Monday please wire.' So now it was *my* series, not his. That was what I got for bragging about being an 'instant market'. So she wired the money instantly, and I got this complaint:

I don't get a word from you except in telegrams. Please do take time to answer this if you possibly can. You have one story of mine 'Between Planes' which doesn't belong to the Pat Hobby series. It is a story that I should hate to see held up for a long time. If your plans are to publish it only at the end of the Pat Hobby series would you consider trading it back to me for the next Pat Hobby story? I might be able to dispose of it elsewhere. Otherwise I very strongly wish that you could schedule it at least as early as to follow the first half dozen Pat Hobbys.

The weakest of the Hobby stories seem to me to have been 'Two Old-Timers' and 'Mightier Than the Sword'. If you could hold those out of type for a while I might be able either to improve them later or else send others in their place. You remember I did this in the case of a story sent you a few years ago.

Answering that, I stuck up for the 'Two Old Timers', and particularly for the moment when the guard, speaking of how soon they may be let out, differentiates between how soon the ex-star may be let out as opposed to how long poor old Pat may be held.

On February 7, 1940, he wrote further:

What would you think of this? You remember that about a week ago I wrote asking about the publication of 'Between Planes'. You said that you hadn't intended to publish it until after the Pat Hobby stories. Why don't you publish it under a pseudonym – say John Darcy. I'm awfully tired of being Scott Fitzgerald anyhow as there doesn't seem to be so much money in it and I'd like to find out if people read me just because I am Scott Fitzgerald or, what is more likely, don't read me for the same reason. In other words it would fascinate me to have one of my stories stand on its own merits completely and see if there is a response. I think it would be a shame to let that story stand over such a long time.

What do you think of this? While the story is not unlike me it is not particularly earmarked by my style as far as I know. At least I don't think so. If the idea interests you I might invent a fictitious personality for Mr Darcy. My ambition would be to get a fan letter from my own daughter.

> Ever your friend,
> John Darcy
> (F. Scott Fitzgerald)

On February 6, 1940, after receipt of a wired advance against it, the twelfth story, 'Pat Hobby and Orson Welles', came in with the request to shove it in the earliest possible issue, and this P.S.:

I've lost track of the order in which I sent you the stories. Would you have one of your slaves write me a note telling me the order in which the stories were received?

This was done, and on Valentine's Day 1940, after a wired advance against it on Lincoln's Birthday, 'On the Trail of Pat Hobby' left Encino with this note:

This is short but it seems to me one of the very funniest of all. I know that is a dangerous thing to say but I think this really has a couple of belly laughs. I wish you could schedule it ahead of 'Pat Hobby's College Days' and put that one last. It seems the weakest of all to me and perhaps I can substitute another one for it later.

This note accompanied 'Pat Hobby's Secret' on March 9, 1940:

I think this one should go in as early as possible (that is if you agree with me that it is one of the best). The strongest should come first in comedy because once a character is really established as funny everything he does becomes funny. At least it's that way in life.

If you agree then, I hope you have this substituted for any of the earlier stories except 'Orson', 'No Harm Trying', or 'Young Visitor'. It is better than any of the others I feel sure.

The old complaint about money accompanied the next,

'Pat Hobby Does His Bit', with this note of March 18, 1940,
enclosing a couple of corrections for it:

I am sorry you can't pay more for the Pat stories. I've gotten
so interested in them that I feel a great deal is going into them.

'Homes of the Stars' followed ten days later, after being
saluted with the usual wired advance:

Hope you like this one. I *think* I am going to work on the picture version of my own story, Babylon Revisited, so this may
be the last Pat story for a couple of months. I think this is good
enough to be shoved ahead of what I indicated in one of my
last letters as the least good of the stories.
  This could come after 'Pat Hobby Does His Bit'.

The most recent list which had downgraded, as 'the less
interesting', a couple of his previous favorites, was com-
prised of the following: 'Two Old Timers', 'Pat Hobby's
Preview', 'On the Trail of Pat Hobby', 'Pat Hobby's College
Days', 'A Patriotic Short', and 'Mightier Than the Sword'.
  Once he tried taking Pat out of Hollywood, eliciting a
wired advance for a story titled 'Pat at the Fair', but wrote
as follows about it on June 14, 1940:

Thanks for the advance. I thought I had a comic idea and have
actually written three versions of it but it simply isn't funny.
Pat out of Hollywood doesn't jell, so I'm doing another Hobby
story which you will get Tuesday. There was no use sending a
poor one.
  Will you tell me what response you're getting from them, or
does anyone care about anything now except the war? Thanks
again for the advance.

On June 25, 1940 came 'Fun in an Artist's Studio' with
this note:

Believe it or not this is the fourth story about Pat in the last
two weeks. One of the others was good but I wanted a story

that would be up to the late ones. It is rather more risque than those in the past – a concession to war times. I hope you can put it ahead of those I have designated in other letters as being mediocre.

You haven't answered my questions about 'Between Planes'. I do wish you would publish it but I wish if it is not already set up that the nom-de-plume could be changed to John Blue instead of John Darcy.

I do hope you can keep this title rather than change it to something with the word Pat in it. In the case of 'Putative Father' changing the title (from 'Young Visitor') anticipated the first climax. If you want to use the word Pat in a subtitle, O.K., but the title is really an intrinsic part of a story, isn't it?

If you like this will you wire the money?

Asking for a pseudonym that didn't sound quite so obviously phony as John Blue brought the following, on July 13, 1940:

My name is Paul Elgin and Paul will presently send you some contributions.

I see that your next scheduled story is 'Pat Hobby Does His Bit' and I hope that the one after that is 'No Harm Trying'. It certainly seems to me next in order of merit. You didn't comment on 'Fun in an Artist's Studio'. Perhaps if your secretary told me in which order the remaining stories are scheduled I might be able to make some changes in one or two of them before they go into type. There are a couple there that don't please me at all.

Paul Elgin did send in a story, called 'On an Ocean Wave', on October 3, and we published it, but by the time it appeared (February '41) Scott was dead, and could never know whether Scottie would write him a fan letter.

Also on October 3 he wrote: 'Deems Taylor paid me a compliment on the Hobby stories the other day. I had about decided that nobody was reading them.'

On October 14, barely two months before his death, he sent off a revise of 'A Patriotic Short', and wired about it the same day:

Revision of 'A Patriotic Short' sent today. Please insert it before any others as far as possible. Plan to revise all that remain. Regards.

As luck would have it, that one was already printed, in an early form for our December 1940 issue, so we had to tell him so, and there was this consequent uproar:

Patriotic short so confused it will stop interest in series stop several people concur in this stop can't you set it up again stop your letter promised to hold it out.

Although the revisions were really minor, he made such an unbuttoned fuss about our inability to accommodate them that we had to draw up a schedule of deadlines on all the remaining stories, setting dates by which revisions would have to be received on the five stories awaiting publication in the issues from January through May 1941. But the last five scenes of the comedy went unrevised. His first heart attack occurred the next month, and two months later, just before Christmas 1940, the second one killed him.

So although he had planned to revise them all, and undoubtedly to shuffle the order of the sequence at least once again, before turning the whole lot in to Scribners as a book, the stories lay where they fell, uncollected and largely ignored, for two lost decades.

There was a rich irony in this that Fitzgerald would have been the first to appreciate. For *Pat Hobby*, a book that he himself had written, went unpublished through successive waves of revival of interest in Fitzgerald. Books *about* Fitzgerald, and even movies and plays, made a lot of money for other people, while this one remaining book *by* Fitzgerald was ignored. As Scott had himself written, there didn't seem to be much money in *being* Scott Fitzgerald, however much there might be in being or becoming an authority *on* Scott Fitzgerald. For Pat Hobby could well say, as he had in the very first story about him to appear in print, 'I've had a hell of a time. I've waited so long.'

He certainly had one hell of a time getting published.

Failure always fascinated Fitzgerald, and he would have felt sardonic satisfaction in having created, in Pat, such a thoroughgoing failure that he couldn't even, so to speak, 'get on the lot' for more than twenty-one years. For while everybody and his ghost began putting between book covers every least and last scrap of Fitzgeraldiana, poor Pat, as the one remaining Fitzgerald 'original', couldn't even get into print.

Scott's own favorite scene in his first book, *This Side of Paradise*, was the one where the boy, showing off for his classmates who watch with bated breath while he opens the envelope in which a pink slip will tell him that he stays in Princeton, or a blue slip that he must leave, waves it and says 'Blue as the sky, gentlemen'.

He would similarly have enjoyed the realization that Pat Hobby became 'a man in the way' – wanting to help and not being allowed to – when the great day came that they began carting off, as museum pieces, literally everything that Scott Fitzgerald had ever touched.

Only Scottie, Fitzgerald's only daughter, had a kind word for poor old Pat, whenever the subject of a separate volume for Pat Hobby came up. 'Why, he sent me to Vassar,' she said.

There you have the ultimate irony. Just as in 'Boil Some Water', while everybody else stood around, Pat alone had acted And of course, as a result, he had to take the rap.

The Pat Hobby stories had been a sore point in the Fitzgerald literary entourage almost from the start. Always most abusive to those who treated him best, though endlessly forbearing to those who treated him badly, Scott had used this series to show Harold Ober, his literary agent, that he *could* get along without him.

Having paid back, during the year and a half that he made good money at MGM, the thousands of dollars that Ober had advanced him out of his own pocket in the lean years memorialized by *The Crack-Up*, Scott began again in 1939, after losing the MGM contract and after the wretched spring that followed the Dartmouth Carnival fiasco, to start assuming that he could again run up unlimited advances at Ober's expense. Ober, the most long-suffering of men and a veritable saint among literary agents, prudently refused to allow himself to be drawn back into the same morass from which he had so lately emerged, and Scott was furious with him. So Scott began again, in the Fall of '39, just as he had ever since '34, every time he had exhausted his credit with Ober, to bypass him and start getting telegraphed advances direct from *Esquire*. Not unnaturally, Pat Hobby became a red flag to Harold Ober.

Nor was Pat Hobby exactly a term of endearment around Maxwell Perkins. He, too, having exhausted what he could do for Scott professionally, through Scribners, had begun dipping into his own pocket, and Scott wasn't above using Pat Hobby to show *him* that he wasn't indispensable.

Since Maxwell Perkins and Harold Ober were the Alpha and Omega of the Fitzgerald literary high command after his death, it was hardly surprising that Pat Hobby's standing at headquarters stayed away down even after Fitzgerald's began to shoot up. But Pat got around that by the simple expedient of outliving them both.

Despite the fact that, as Fitzgerald himself had said, he had become so interested in the Pat Hobby stories that he felt a great deal was going into them, they were for a long time dismissed as being 'done to pay the grocer'. It is true that, except for odd studio jobs, they constituted his only certain source of income in those last two years, and they were written to redeem a spate of fifty and hundred dollar advances made by wire to the bank at Culver City. But to counterbalance that consideration, the thing to remember is that Scott Fitzgerald wrote for his living all the twenty years of his working life.

From 1920 on he wrote for money – enough to marry Zelda in the first place and to afford her, and the wild life they led together until 1930. And after that, he wrote for money enough to meet the strain of her fantastically expensive treatments for mental illness. So in a very real sense it could be said that Fitzgerald wrote for his living, as opposed to living for his work, more than any other author of our time. In fact, paradoxically, if ever he could have been said to be living for his work, it was in his Pat Hobby period, those last two desperately difficult years of his life.

But after Scott's death, almost from the moment the papers were first made available in the Princeton Library, the scholars began falling, with singular uniformity, into the pathetic fallacy about Pat Hobby: these stories are about a hack, *ergo* these stories are hack work. But Pat will ultimately have his way even there. For some time the scholars will have a field day, going through the successive layers of revision of the various Pat Hobby stories, like so many palimpsests.

For the purposes of the present volume, however, it will suffice to give the single exhibit of the revision of 'A Patriotic Short', to show how much importance Fitzgerald could attach to relatively minor changes in the text of one of these stories. This was the one that he feared would 'stop interest in the series' if we printed it without this revision, because it was 'so confused'. You can see for yourself that it isn't. And the fact that you can shows that it didn't.

For with this volume, an authentic first edition, however belated, the Fitzgerald cast of major characters is at last complete, and Pat Hobby takes his rightful place, if not alongside Jay Gatsby and Dick Diver, then at least between Monroe Stahr and Amory Blaine.

Arnold Gingrich

March 7 1962
New York, N.Y.

Pat Hobby's Christmas Wish

It was Christmas Eve in the studio. By eleven o'clock in the morning. Santa Claus had called on most of the huge population according to each one's deserts.

Sumptuous gifts from producers to stars, and from agents to producers arrived at offices and studio bungalows: on every stage one heard of the roguish gifts of casts to directors or directors to casts; champagne had gone out from publicity office to the press. And tips of fifties, tens and fives from producers, directors and writers fell like manna upon the white collar class.

In this sort of transaction there were exceptions. Pat Hobby, for example, who knew the game from twenty years' experience, had had the idea of getting rid of his secretary the day before. They were sending over a new one any minute – but she would scarcely expect a present the first day.

Waiting for her, he walked the corridor, glancing into open offices for signs of life. He stopped to chat with Joe Hopper from the scenario department.

'Not like the old days,' he mourned. 'Then there was a bottle on every desk.'

'There're a few around.'

'Not many.' Pat sighed. 'And afterwards we'd run a picture – made up out of cutting-room scraps.'

'I've heard. All the suppressed stuff,' said Hopper.

Pat nodded, his eyes glistening.

'Oh, it was juicy. You darned near ripped your guts laughing – '

He broke off as the sight of a woman, pad in hand, entering his office down the hall recalled him to the sorry present.

'Gooddorf has me working over the holiday,' he complained bitterly.

'I wouldn't do it.'

'I wouldn't either except my four weeks are up next Friday, and if I bucked him he wouldn't extend me.'

As he turned away Hopper knew that Pat was not being extended anyhow. He had been hired to script an old-fashioned horse-opera and the boys who were 'writing behind him' – that is working over his stuff – said that all of it was old and some didn't make sense.

'I'm Miss Kagle,' said Pat's new secretary.

She was about thirty-six, handsome, faded, tired, efficient. She went to the typewriter, examined it, sat down and burst into sobs.

Pat started. Self-control, from below anyhow, was the rule around here. Wasn't it bad enough to be working on Christmas Eve ? Well – less bad than not working at all. He walked over and shut the door – someone might suspect him of insulting the girl.

'Cheer up,' he advised her. 'This is Christmas.'

Her burst of emotion had died away. She sat upright now, choking and wiping her eyes.

'Nothing's as bad as it seems,' he assured her unconvincingly. 'What's it, anyhow ? They going to lay you off ?'

She shook her head, did a sniffle to end sniffles, and opened her note book.

'Who you been working for ?'

She answered between suddenly gritted teeth.

'Mr Harry Gooddorf.'

Pat widened his permanently bloodshot eyes. Now he remembered he had seen her in Harry's outer office.

'Since 1921. Eighteen years. And yesterday he sent me back to the department. He said I depressed him – I reminded him he was getting on.' Her face was grim. 'That isn't the way he talked after hours eighteen years ago.'

'Yeah, he was a skirt chaser then,' said Pat.

'I should have done something then when I had the chance.'

Pat felt righteous stirrings.

'Breach of promise? That's no angle!'

'But I had something to clinch it. Something bigger than breach of promise. I still have too. But then, you see, I thought I was in love with him.' She brooded for a moment. 'Do you want to dictate something now?'

Pat remembered his job and opened a script.

'It's an insert,' he began. 'Scene 114 A.'

Pat paced the office.

'Ext. Long Shot of the Plains,' he decreed. 'Buck and Mexicans approaching the hyacenda.'

'The what?'

'The hyacenda – the ranch house.' He looked at her reproachfully. '114 B. Two Shot: Buck and Pedro. Buck: "The dirty son-of-a-bitch. I'll tear his guts out!" '

Miss Kagle looked up, startled.

'You want me to write that down?'

'Sure.'

'It won't get by.'

'I'm writing this. Of course, it won't get by. But if I put "you rat" the scene won't have any force.'

'But won't somebody have to change it to "you rat"?'

He glared at her – he didn't want to change secretaries every day.

'Harry Gooddorf can worry about that.'

'Are you working for Mr Gooddorf?' Miss Kagle asked in alarm.

'Until he throws me out.'

'I shouldn't have said – '

'Don't worry,' he assured her. 'He's no pal of mine anymore. Not at three-fifty a week, when I used to get two thousand . . . Where was I?'

He paced the floor again, repeating his last line aloud with relish. But now it seemed to apply not to a personage of the story but to Harry Gooddorf. Suddenly he stood still, lost in thought. 'Say, what is it you got on him? You know where the body is buried?'

'That's too true to be funny.'

'He knock somebody off?'

'Mr Hobby, I'm sorry I ever opened my mouth.'

'Just call me Pat. What's your first name?'

'Helen.'

'Married?'

'Not now.'

'Well, listen Helen: What do you say we have dinner?'

II

On the afternoon of Christmas Day he was still trying to get the secret out of her. They had the studio almost to themselves – only a skeleton staff of technical men dotted the walks and the commissary. They had exchanged Christmas presents. Pat gave her a five dollar bill, Helen bought him a white linen handkerchief. Very well he could remember the day when many dozen such handkerchiefs had been his Christmas harvest.

The script was progressing at a snail's pace but their friendship had considerably ripened. Her secret, he considered, was a very valuable asset, and he wondered how many careers had turned on just such an asset. Some, he felt sure, had been thus raised to affluence. Why, it was almost as good as being in the family, and he pictured an imaginary conversation with Harry Gooddorf.

'Harry, it's this way. I don't think my experience is being made use of. It's the young squirts who ought to do the writing – I ought to do more supervising.'

'Or – ?'

'Or else,' said Pat firmly.

He was in the midst of his day dream when Harry Gooddorf unexpectedly walked in.

'Merry Christmas, Pat,' he said jovially. His smile was less robust when he saw Helen, 'Oh, hello Helen – didn't know you and Pat had got together. I sent you a remembrance over to the script department.'

'You shouldn't have done that.'

Harry turned swiftly to Pat.

'The boss is on my neck,' he said. 'I've got to have a finished script Thursday.'

'Well, here I am,' said Pat. 'You'll have it. Did I ever fail you?'

'Usually,' said Harry. 'Usually.'

He seemed about to add more when a call boy entered with an envelope and handed it to Helen Kagle – whereupon Harry turned and hurried out.

'He'd better get out!' burst forth Miss Kagle, after opening the envelope. 'Ten bucks – just *ten bucks* – from an executive – after eighteen years.'

It was Pat's chance. Sitting on her desk he told her his plan.

'It's soft jobs for you and me,' he said. 'You the head of a script department, me an associate producer. We're on the gravy train for life – no more writing – no more pounding the keys. We might even – we might even – if things go good we could get married.'

She hesitated a long time. When she put a fresh sheet in the typewriter Pat feared he had lost.

'I can write it from memory,' she said. 'This was a letter he typed *himself* on February 3rd, 1921. He sealed it and gave it to me to mail – but there was a blonde he was interested in, and I wondered why he should be so secret about a letter.'

Helen had been typing as she talked, and now she handed Pat a note.

To Will Bronson
First National Studios
   Personal
Dear Bill:
   We killed Taylor. We should have cracked down on him sooner. So why not shut up.

                                                    Yours, Harry

Pat stared at it stunned.

'Get it?' Helen said. 'On February 1st, 1921, somebody knocked off William Desmond Taylor, the director. And they've never found out who.'

III

For eighteen years she had kept the original note, envelope and all. She had sent only a copy to Bronson, tracing Harry Gooddorf's signature.

'Baby, we're set!' said Pat. 'I always thought it was a *girl* got Taylor.'

He was so elated that he opened a drawer and brought forth a half-pint of whiskey. Then, with an afterthought, he demanded:

'Is it in a safe place?'

'You bet it is. He'd never guess where.'

'Baby, we've got him!'

Cash, cars, girls, swimming pools swam in a glittering montage before Pat's eye.

He folded the note, put it in his pocket, took another drink and reached for his hat.

'You going to see him now?' Helen demanded in some alarm. 'Hey, wait till I get off the lot. *I* don't want to get murdered.'

'Don't worry! Listen I'll meet you in "The Muncherie" at Fifth and La Brea – in one hour.'

As he walked to Gooddorf's office he decided to mention no facts or names within the walls of the studio. Back in the brief period when he had headed a scenario department Pat had conceived a plan to put a dictaphone in every writer's office. Thus their loyalty to the studio executives could be checked several times a day.

The idea had been laughed at. But later, when he had been 'reduced back to a writer', he often wondered if his plan was secretly followed. Perhaps some indiscreet remark of his own was responsible for the doghouse where he had been interred for the past decade. So it was with the idea of concealed dictaphones in mind, dictaphones which could be turned on by the pressure of a toe, that he entered Harry Gooddorf's office.

'Harry – ' he chose his words carefully, 'do you remember the night of February 1st, 1921?'

Somewhat flabbergasted, Gooddorf leaned back in his swivel chair.

'*What?*'

'Try and think. It's something very important to you.'

Pat's expression as he watched his friend was that of an anxious undertaker.

'February 1st, 1921.' Gooddorf mused. 'No. How could I remember? You think I keep a diary? I don't even know where I was then.'

'You were right here in Hollywood.'

'Probably. If you know, tell me.'

'You'll remember.'

'Let's see. I came out to the coast in sixteen. I was with Biograph till 1920. Was I making some comedies? That's it. I was making a piece called *Knuckleduster* – on location.'

'You weren't always on location. You were in town February 1st.'

'What is this?' Gooddorf demanded. 'The third degree?'

'No – but I've got some information about your doings on that date.'

Gooddorf's face reddened; for a moment it looked as if he were going to throw Pat out of the room – then suddenly he gasped, licked his lips and stared at his desk.

'Oh,' he said, and after a minute: 'But I don't see what business it is of yours.'

'It's the business of every decent man.'

'Since when have you been decent?'

'All my life,' said Pat. 'And, even if I haven't, I never did anything like that.'

'My foot!' said Harry contemptuously. '*You* showing up here with a halo! Anyhow, what's the evidence? You'd think you had a written confession. It's all forgotten long ago.'

'Not in the memory of decent men,' said Pat. 'And as for a written confession – I've got it.'

'I doubt you. And I doubt if it would stand in any court. You've been taken in.'

'I've seen it,' said Pat with growing confidence. 'And it's enough to hang you.'

'Well, by God if there's any publicity I'll run you out of town.'

'You'll run *me* out of town.'

'I don't want any publicity.'

'Then I think you'd better come along with me. Without talking to anybody.'

'Where are we going?'

'I know a bar where we can be alone.'

The Muncherie was in fact deserted, save for the bar-
tender and Helen Kagle who sat at a table, jumpy with
alarm. Seeing her, Gooddorf's expression changed to one
of infinite reproach.

'This is a hell of a Christmas,' he said, 'with my family
expecting me home an hour ago. I want to know the idea.
You say you've got something in my writing.'

Pat took the paper from his pocket and read the date
aloud. Then he looked up hastily:

'This is just a copy, so don't try and snatch it.'

He knew the technique of such scenes as this. When the
vogue for Westerns had temporarily subsided he had
sweated over many an orgy of crime.

'To William Bronson, Dear Bill: We killed Taylor. We
should have cracked down on him sooner. So why not
shut up. Yours, Harry.'

Pat paused. 'You wrote this on February 3rd, 1921.'

Silence. Gooddorf turned to Helen Kagle.

'Did *you* do this? Did I dictate that to you?'

'No,' she admitted in an awed voice. 'You wrote it yourself. I opened the letter.'

'I see. Well, what do you want?'

'Plenty,' said Pat, and found himself pleased with the
sound of the word.

'What exactly?'

Pat launched into the description of a career suitable to
a man of forty-nine. A glowing career. It expanded rapidly
in beauty and power during the time it took him to drink
three large whiskeys. But one demand he returned to again
and again.

He wanted to be made a producer tomorrow.

'Why tomorrow?' demanded Gooddorf. 'Can't it wait?'

There were sudden tears in Pat's eyes – real tears.

'This is Christmas,' he said. 'It's my Christmas wish. I've had a hell of a time. I've waited so long.'

Gooddorf got to his feet suddenly.

'Nope,' he said. 'I won't make you a producer. I couldn't do it in fairness to the company. I'd rather stand trial.'

Pat's mouth fell open.

'What? You won't?'

'Not a chance. I'd rather swing.'

He turned away, his face set, and started toward the door.

'All right!' Pat called after him. 'It's your last chance.'

Suddenly he was amazed to see Helen Kagle spring up and run after Gooddorf – try to throw her arms around him.

'Don't worry!' she cried. 'I'll tear it up, Harry! It was a joke Harry –'

Her voice trailed off rather abruptly. She had discovered that Gooddorf was shaking with laughter.

'What's the joke?' she demanded, growing angry again. 'Do you think I haven't got it?'

'Oh, you've got it all right,' Gooddorf howled. 'You've got it – but it isn't what you think it is.'

He came back to the table, sat down and addressed Pat.

'Do you know what I thought that date meant? I thought maybe it was the date Helen and I first fell for each other. That's what I thought. And I thought she was going to raise Cain about it. I thought she was nuts. She's been married twice since then, and so have I.'

'That doesn't explain the note,' said Pat sternly but with a sinky feeling. 'You admit you killed Taylor.'

Gooddorf nodded.

'I still think a lot of us did,' he said. 'We were a wild crowd – Taylor and Bronson and me and half the boys in the big money. So a bunch of us got together in an agreement to go slow. The country was waiting for somebody to hang. We tried to get Taylor to watch his step but he wouldn't. So instead of cracking down on him, we let him "go the pace". And some rat shot him – who did it I don't know.'

He stood up.

'Like somebody should have cracked down on *you*, Pat. But you were an amusing guy in those days, and besides we were all too busy.'

Pat sniffled suddenly.

'I've *been* cracked down on,' he said. 'Plenty.'

'But too late,' said Gooddorf, and added, 'you've probably got a new Christmas wish by now, and I'll grant it to you. I won't say anything about this afternoon.'

When he had gone, Pat and Helen sat in silence. Presently Pat took out the note again and looked it over.

' "So why not shut up?" ' he read aloud. 'He didn't explain that.'

'Why *not* shut up?' Helen said.

A Man in the Way

Pat Hobby could always get on the lot. He had worked there fifteen years on and off – chiefly off during the past five – and most of the studio police knew him. If tough customers on watch asked to see his studio card he could get in by phoning Lou, the bookie. For Lou also, the studio had been home for many years.

Pat was forty-nine. He was a writer but he had never written much, nor even read all the 'originals' he worked from, because it made his head bang to read much. But the good old silent days you got somebody's plot and a smart secretary and gulped benzedrine 'structure' at her six or eight hours every week. The director took care of the gags. After talkies came he always teamed up with some man who wrote dialogue. Some young man who liked to work.

'I've got a list of credits second to none,' he told Jack Berners. 'All I need is an idea and to work with somebody who isn't all wet.'

He had buttonholed Jack outside the production office as Jack was going to lunch and they walked together in the direction of the commissary.

'You bring *me* an idea,' said Jack Berners. 'Things are tight. We can't put a man on salary unless he's got an idea.'

'How can you get ideas off salary ?' Pat demanded – then he added hastily: 'Anyhow I got the germ of an idea that I could be telling you all about at lunch.'

Something might come to him at lunch. There was Baer's notion about the boy scout. But Jack said cheerfully:

'I've got a date for lunch, Pat. Write it out and send it around, eh?'

He felt cruel because he knew Pat couldn't write anything out but he was having story trouble himself. The war had just broken out and every producer on the lot wanted to end their current stories with the hero going to war. And Jack Berners felt he had thought of that first for his production.

'So write it out, eh?'

When Pat didn't answer Jack looked at him – he saw a sort of whipped misery in Pat's eye that reminded him of his own father. Pat had been in the money before Jack was out of college – with three cars and a chicken over every garage. Now his clothes looked as if he'd been standing at Hollywood and Vine for three years.

'Scout around and talk to some of the writers on the lot,' he said. 'If you can get one of them interested in your idea, bring him up to see me.'

'I hate to give an idea without money on the line,' Pat brooded pessimistically. 'These young squirts'll lift the shirt off your back.'

They had reached the commissary door.

'Good luck, Pat. Anyhow we're not in Poland.'

– Good *you're* not, said Pat under his breath. They'd slit your gizzard.

Now what to do? He went up and wandered along the cell block of writers. Almost everyone had gone to lunch and those who were in he didn't know. Always there were more and more unfamiliar faces. And he had thirty credits; he had been in the business, publicity and script-writing, for twenty years.

The last door in the line belonged to a man he didn't like.

But he wanted a place to sit a minute so with a knock he pushed it open. The man wasn't there – only a very pretty, frail-looking girl sat reading a book.

'I think he's left Hollywood,' she said in answer to his question. 'They gave me his office but they forgot to put up my name.'

'You a writer ?' Pat asked in surprise.

'I work at it.'

'You ought to get 'em to give you a test.'

'No – I like writing.'

'What's that you're reading.'

She showed him.

'Let me give you a tip,' he said. 'That's not the way to get the guts out of a book.'

'Oh.'

'I've been here for years – I'm Pat Hobby – and I *know*. Give the book to four of your friends to read it. Get them to tell you what stuck in their minds. Write it down and you've got a picture -- see ?'

The girl smiled.

'Well, that's very – very original advice, Mr Hobby.'

'Pat Hobby,' he said. 'Can I wait here a minute ? Man I came to see is at lunch.'

He sat down across from her and picked up a copy of a photo magazine.

'Oh, just let me mark that,' she said quickly.

He looked at the page which she checked. It showed paintings being boxed and carted away to safety from an art gallery in Europe.

'How'll you use it ?' he said.

'Well, I thought it would be dramatic if there was an old man around while they were packing the pictures. A poor old man, trying to get a job helping them. But they can't use him – he's in the way – not even good cannon fodder. They want strong young people in the world. And it turns out he's the man who painted the pictures many years ago.'

Pat considered.

'It's good but I don't get it,' he said.

'Oh, it's nothing, a short short maybe.'

'Got any good picture ideas? I'm in with all the markets here.'

'I'm under contract.'

'Use another name.'

Her phone rang.

'Yes, this is Pricilla Smith,' the girl said.

After a minute she turned to Pat.

'Will you excuse me? This is a private call.'

He got it and walked out, and along the corridor. Finding an office with no name on it he went in and fell asleep on the couch.

II

Late that afternoon he returned to Jack Berners' waiting rooms. He had an idea about a man who meets a girl in an office and he thinks she's a stenographer but she turns out to be a writer. He engages her as a stenographer, though, and they start for the South Seas. It was a beginning, it was something to tell Jack, he thought – and, picturing Pricilla Smith, he refurbished some old business he hadn't seen used for years.

He became quite excited about it – felt quite young for a moment and walked up and down the waiting room mentally rehearsing the first sequence. 'So here we have a situation like *It Happened One Night* – only *new*. I see Hedy Lamarr – '

Oh, he knew how to talk to these boys if he could get to them, with something to say.

'Mr Berners still busy?' he asked for the fifth time.

'Oh, yes, Mr Hobby. Mr Bill Costello and Mr Bach are in there.'

He thought quickly. It was half-past five. In the old days he had just busted in sometimes and sold an idea, an idea good for a couple of grand because it was just the moment when they were very tired of what they were doing at present.

He walked innocently out and to another door in the hall. He knew it led through a bathroom right in to Jack Berners' office. Drawing a quick breath he plunged . . .

'. . . So that's the notion,' he concluded after five minutes. 'It's just a flash – nothing really worked out, but you could give me an office and a girl and I could have something on paper for you in three days.'

Berners, Costello and Bach did not even have to look at each other. Berners spoke for them all as he said firmly and gently:

'That's no idea, Pat. I can't put you on salary for that.'

'Why don't you work it out further by yourself,' suggeted Bill Costello. 'And then let's see it. We're looking for ideas – especially about the war.'

'A man can think better on salary,' said Pat.

There was silence. Costello and Bach had drunk with him, played poker with him, gone to the races with him. They'd honestly be glad to see him placed.

'The war, eh,' he said gloomily. 'Everything is war now, no matter how many credits a man has. Do you know what it makes me think of? It makes me think of a well-known painter in the discard. It's war time and he's use-less – just a man in the way.' He warmed to his concep-tion of himself, ' – but all the time they're carting away *his own paintings* as the most valuable thing worth saving.

And they won't even let me help. That's what it reminds me of.'

There was again silence for a moment.

'That isn't a bad idea,' said Bach thoughtfully. He turned to the others. 'You know ? In itself ?'

Bill Costello nodded.

'Not bad at all. And I know where we could spot it. Right at the end of the fourth sequence. We just change old Ames to a painter.'

Presently they talked money.

'I'll give you two weeks on it,' said Berners to Pat. 'At two-fifty.'

'Two-fifty!' objected Pat. 'Say there was one time you paid me ten times that!'

'That was ten years ago,' Jack reminded him. 'Sorry. Best we can do now.'

'You make me feel like that old painter – '

'Don't oversell it,' said Jack, rising and smiling. 'You're on the payroll.'

Pat went out with a quick step and confidence in his eyes. Half a grand – that would take the pressure off for a month and you could often stretch two weeks into three – sometimes four. He left the studio proudly through the front entrance, stopping at the liquor store for a half-pint to take back to his room.

By seven o'clock things were even better. Santa Anita tomorrow, if he could get an advance. And tonight – something festive ought to be done tonight. With a sudden rush of pleasure he went down to the phone in the lower hall, called the studio and asked for Miss Pricilla Smith's number. He hadn't met anyone so pretty for years . . .

In her apartment Pricilla Smith spoke rather firmly into the phone.

'I'm awfully sorry,' she said, 'but I couldn't possibly . . . No – and I'm tied up all the rest of the week.'

As she hung up, Jack Berners spoke from the couch.

'Who was it?'

'Oh, some man who came in the office,' she laughed, 'and told me never to read the story I was working on.'

'Shall I believe you?'

'You certainly shall. I'll even think of his name in a minute. But first I want to tell you about an idea I had this morning. I was looking at a photo in a magazine where they were packing up some works of art in the Tate Gallery in London. And I thought – '

'Boil Some Water – Lots of It'

Pat Hobby sat in his office in the writers' building and looked at his morning's work, just come back from the script department. He was on a 'polish job', about the only kind he ever got nowadays. He was to repair a messy sequence in a hurry, but the word 'hurry' neither frightened nor inspired him for Pat had been in Hollywood since he was thirty – now he was forty-nine. All the work he had done this morning (except a little changing around of lines so he could claim them as his own) – all he had actually invented was a single imperative sentence, spoken by a doctor.

'Boil some water – lots of it.'

It was a good line. It had sprung into his mind full grown as soon as he had read the script. In the old silent days Pat would have used it as a spoken title and ended his dialogue worries for a space, but he needed some spoken words for other people in the scene. Nothing came.

'Boil some water,' he repeated to himself. 'Lot's of it.'

The word boil brought a quick glad thought of the commissary. A reverent thought too – for an old-timer like Pat, what people you sat with at lunch was more important in getting along than what you dictated in your office. This was no art, as he often said – this was an industry.

'This is no art,' he remarked to Max Leam who was leisurely drinking at a corridor water cooler. 'This is an industry.'

Max had flung him this timely bone of three weeks at three-fifty.

'Say look, Pat! Have you got anything down on paper yet?'

'Say I've got some stuff already that'll make 'em – ' He named a familiar biological function with the somewhat startling assurance that it would take place in the theatre.

Max tried to gauge his sincerity.

'Want to read it to me now?' he asked.

'Not yet. But it's got the old guts if you know what I mean.'

Max was full of doubts.

'Well, go to it. And if you run into any medical snags check with the doctor over at the First Aid Station. It's got to be right.'

The spirit of Pasteur shone firmly in Pat's eyes.

'It will be.'

He felt good walking across the lot with Max – so good that he decided to glue himself to the producer and sit down with him at the Big Table. But Max foiled his intention by cooing 'See you later' and slipping into the barber shop.

Once Pat had been a familiar figure at the Big Table; often in his golden prime he had dined in the private canteens of executives. Being of the older Hollywood he understood their jokes, their vanities, their social system with its swift fluctuations. But there were too many new faces at the Big Table now – faces that looked at him with the universal Hollywood suspicion. And at the little tables where the young writers sat they seemed to take work so seriously. As for just sitting down anywhere, even with secretaries or extras – Pat would rather catch a sandwich at the corner.

Detouring to the Red Cross Station he asked for the

doctor. A girl, a nurse, answered from a wall mirror where she was hastily drawing her lips, 'He's out. What is it?'

'Oh. Then I'll come back.'

She had finished, and now she turned – vivid and young and with a bright consoling smile.

'Miss Stacey will help you. I'm about to go to lunch.'

He was aware of an old, old feeling – left over from the time when he had had wives – a feeling that to invite this little beauty to lunch might cause trouble. But he remembered quickly that he didn't have any wives now – they had both given up asking for alimony.

'I'm working on a medical,' he said. 'I need some help.'

'A medical?'

'Writing it – idea about a doc. Listen – let me buy you lunch. I want to ask you some medical questions.'

The nurse hesitated.

'I don't know. It's my first day out here.'

'It's all right,' he assured her, 'studios are democratic; everybody is just "Joe" or "Mary" – from the big shots right down to the prop boys.'

He proved it magnificently on their way to lunch by greeting a male star and getting his own name back in return. And in the commissary, where they were placed hard by the Big Table, his producer, Max Leam, looked up, did a little 'takem' and winked.

The nurse – her name was Helen Earle – peered about eagerly.

'I don't see anybody,' she said. 'Except oh, there's Ronald Colman. I didn't know Ronald Colman looked like that.'

Pat pointed suddenly to the floor.

'And there's Mickey Mouse!'

She jumped and Pat laughed at his joke – but Helen Earle was already staring starry-eyed at the costume extras who filled the hall with the colors of the First Empire. Pat was piqued to see her interest go out to these nonentities.

'The big shots are at this next table,' he said solemnly, wistfully, 'directors and all except the biggest executives. They could have Ronald Colman pressing pants. I usually sit over there but they don't want ladies. At lunch, that is, they don't want ladies.'

'Oh,' said Helen Earle, polite but unimpressed. 'It must be wonderful to be a writer too. It's so very interesting.'

'It has its points,' he said . . . he had thought for years it was a dog's life.

'What is it you want to ask me about a doctor ?'

Here was toil again. Something in Pat's mind snapped off when he thought of the story.

'Well, Max Leam – that man facing us – Max Leam and I have a script about a Doc. You know ? Like a hospital picture ?'

'I know.' And she added after a moment, 'That's the reason that I went in training.'

'And we've got to have it *right* because a hundred million people would check on it. So this doctor in the script he tells them to boil some water. He says, "Boil some water – lots of it." And we were wondering what the people would do then.'

'Why – they'd probably boil it,' Helen said, and then, somewhat confused by the question, 'What people ?'

'Well, somebody's daughter and the man that lived there and an attorney and the man that was hurt.'

Helen tried to digest this before answering.

' – and some other guy I'm going to cut out,' he finished.

There was a pause. The waitress set down tuna fish sandwiches.

'Well, when a doctor gives orders they're orders,' Helen decided.

'Hm.' Pat's interest had wandered to an odd little scene at the Big Table while he inquired absently, 'You married?'

'No.'

'Neither am I.'

Beside the Big Table stood an extra. A Russian Cossack with a fierce moustache. He stood resting his hand on the back of an empty chair between Director Paterson and Producer Leam.

'Is this taken?' he asked, with a thick Central European accent.

All along the Big Table faces stared suddenly at him. Until after the first look the supposition was that he must be some well-known actor. But he was not – he was dressed in one of the many-colored uniforms that dotted the room.

Someone at the table said: 'That's taken.' But the man drew out the chair and sat down.

'Got to eat somewhere,' he remarked with a grin.

A shiver went over the near-by tables. Pat Hobby stared with his mouth ajar. It was as if someone had crayoned Donald Duck into the *Last Supper*.

'Look at that,' he advised Helen. 'What they'll do to him! Boy!'

The flabbergasted silence at the Big Table was broken by Ned Harman, the Production Manager.

'This table is reserved,' he said.

The extra looked up from a menu.

'They told me sit anywhere.'

He beckoned a waitress – who hesitated, looking for an answer in the faces of her superiors.

'Extras don't eat here,' said Max Leam, still politely. 'This is a –'

'I got to eat,' said the Cossack doggedly. 'I been standing around six hours while they shoot this stinking mess and now I got to eat.'

The silence had extended – from Pat's angle all within range seemed to be poised in mid-air.

The extra shook his head wearily.

'I dunno who cooked it up – ' he said – and Max Leam sat forward in his chair – 'but it's the lousiest tripe I ever seen shot in Hollywood.'

– At his table Pat was thinking why didn't they do something? Knock him down, drag him away. If they were yellow themselves they could call the studio police.

'Who is that?' Helen Earle was following his eyes innocently. 'Somebody I ought to know?'

He was listening attentively to Max Leam's voice, raised in anger.

'Get up and get out of here, buddy, and get out quick!'

The extra frowned.

'Who's telling me?' he demanded.

'You'll see.' Max appealed to the table at large, 'Where's Cushman – where's the Personnel man?'

'You try to move me,' said the extra, lifting the hilt of his scabbard above the level of the table, 'and I'll hang this on your ear. I know my rights.'

The dozen men at the table, representing a thousand dollars an hour in salaries, sat stunned. Far down by the door one of the studio police caught wind of what was happening and started to elbow through the crowded room. And Big Jack Wilson, another director, was on his feet in an instant coming around the table.

But they were too late – Pat Hobby could stand no more. He had jumped up, seizing a big heavy tray from the serving stand nearby. In two springs he reached the scene of action – lifting the tray he brought it down upon the extra's head with all the strength of his forty-nine years. The extra, who had been in the act of rising to meet Wilson's threatened assault, got the blow full on his face and temple and as he collapsed a dozen red streaks sprang into sight through the heavy grease paint. He crashed sideways between the chairs.

Pat stood over him panting – the tray in his hand.

'The dirty rat!' he cried. 'Where does he think – '

The studio policeman pushed past; Wilson pushed past – the two aghast men from another table rushed up to survey the situation.

'It was a gag!' one of them shouted. 'That's Walter Herrick, the writer. It's his picture.'

'My God!'

'He was kidding Max Leam. It was a gag I tell you!'

'Pull him out ... Get a doctor ... Look out, there!'

Now Helen Earle hurried over; Walter Herrick was dragged out into a cleared space on the floor and there were yells of 'Who did it ? – Who beaned him ?'

Pat let the tray lapse to a chair, its sound unnoticed in the confusion.

He saw Helen Earle working swiftly at the man's head with a pile of clean napkins.

'Why did they have to do this to him ?' someone shouted.

Pat caught Max Leam's eye but Max happened to look away at the moment and a sense of injustice came over Pat. He alone in this crisis, real or imaginary, had *acted*. He alone had played the man, while those stuffed shirts let themselves be insulted and abused. And now he would have to take the rap – because Walter Herrick was powerful and popular, a three thousand a week man who wrote hit shows in New York. How could anyone have guessed that it was a gag ?

There was a doctor now. Pat saw him say something to the manageress and her shrill voice sent the waitresses scattering like leaves toward the kitchen.

'Boil some water! Lots of it!'

The words fell wild and unreal on Pat's burdened soul. But even though he now knew at first hand what came next, he did not think that he could go on from there.

Teamed with Genius

'I took a chance in sending for you,' said Jack Berners. 'But there's a job that you just *may* be able to help out with.'

Though Pat Hobby was not offended, either as man or writer, a formal protest was called for.

'I been in the industry fifteen years, Jack. I've got more screen credits than a dog has got fleas.'

'Maybe I chose the wrong word,' said Jack. 'What I mean is, that was a long time ago. About money we'll pay you just what Republic paid you last month – three-fifty a week. Now – did you ever hear of a writer named René Wilcox?'

The name was unfamiliar. Pat had scarcely opened a book in a decade.

'She's pretty good,' he ventured.

'It's a man, an English playwright. He's only here in L.A. for his health. Well – we've had a Russian Ballet picture kicking around for a year – three bad scripts on it. So last week we signed up René Wilcox – he seemed just the person.'

Pat considered.

'You mean he's – '

'I don't know and I don't care,' interrupted Berners sharply. 'We think we can borrow Zorina, so we want to hurry things up – do a shooting script instead of just a treatment. Wilcox is inexperienced and that's where you come in. You used to be a good man for structure.'

'*Used* to be!'

'All right, maybe you still are.' Jack beamed with momentary encouragement, 'Find yourself an office and get together with René Wilcox.' As Pat started out he called him back and put a bill in his hand. 'First of all, get a new hat. You used to be quite a boy around the secretaries in the old days. Don't give up at forty-nine!'

Over in the Writers' Building Pat glanced at the directory in the hall and knocked at the door of 216. No answer, but he went in to discover a blond, willowy youth of twenty-five staring moodily out the window.

'Hello, René!' Pat said. 'I'm your partner.'

Wilcox's regard questioned even his existence, but Pat continued heartily. 'I hear we're going to lick some stuff into shape. Ever collaborate before?'

'I have never written for the cinema before.'

While this increased Pat's chance for a screen credit he badly needed, it meant that he might have to do some work. The very thought made him thirsty.

'This is different from playwriting,' he suggested, with suitable gravity.

'Yes – I read a book about it.'

Pat wanted to laugh. In 1928 he and another man had concocted such a sucker-trap, *Secrets of Film Writing*. It would have made money if pictures hadn't started to talk.

'It all seems simple enough,' said Wilcox. Suddenly he took his hat from the rack, 'I'll be running along now.'

'Don't you want to talk about the script?' demanded Pat. 'What have you done so far?'

'I've not done anything,' said Wilcox deliberately. 'That idiot, Berners, gave me some trash and told me to go on from there. But it's too dismal.' His blue eyes narrowed, 'I say, what's a boom shot?'

'A boom shot? Why, that's when the camera's on a crane.'

Pat leaned over the desk and picked up a blue-jacketed 'Treatment'. On the cover he read:

BALLET SHOES
A Treatment
by
Consuela Martin
An Original from an idea by Consuela Martin

Pat glanced at the beginning and then at the end.

'I'd like it better if we could get the war in somewhere,' he said frowning. 'Have the dancer go as a Red Cross nurse and then she could get regenerated. See what I mean ?'

There was no answer. Pat turned and saw the door softly closing.

What is this ? he exclaimed. What kind of collaborating can a man do if he walks out ? Wilcox had not even given the legitimate excuse – the races at Santa Anita!

The door opened again, a pretty girl's face, rather frightened, showed itself momentarily, said 'Oh', and disappeared. Then it returned.

'Why it's Mr Hobby!' she exclaimed. 'I was looking for Mr Wilcox.'

He fumbled for her name but she supplied it.

'Katherine Hodge. I was your secretary when I worked here three years ago.'

Pat knew she had once worked with him, but for the moment could not remember whether there had been a deeper relation. It did not seem to him that it had been love – but looking at her now, that appeared rather too bad.

'Sit down,' said Pat. 'You assigned to Wilcox ?'

'I thought so – but he hasn't give me any work yet.'

'I think he's nuts,' Pat said gloomily. 'He asked me what a boom shot was. Maybe he's sick – that's why he's out here. He'll probably start throwing up all over the office.'

'He's well now,' Katherine ventured.

'He doesn't look like it to me. Come on in my office. You can work for *me* this afternoon.'

Pat lay on his couch while Miss Katherine Hodge read the script of *Ballet Shoes* aloud to him. About midway in the second sequence he fell asleep with his new hat on his chest.

II

Except for the hat, that was the identical position in which he found René next day at eleven. And it was that way for three straight days – one was asleep or else the other – and sometimes both. On the fourth day they had several conferences in which Pat again put forward his idea about the war as a regenerating force for ballet dancers.

'Couldn't we *not* talk about the war?' suggested René. 'I have two brothers in the Guards.'

'You're lucky to be here in Hollywood.'

'That's as it may be.'

'Well, what's your idea of the start of the picture?'

'I do not like the present beginning. It gives me an almost physical nausea.'

'So then, we got to have something in its place. That's why I want to plant the war –'

'I'm late to luncheon,' said René Wilcox. 'Good-bye, Mike.'

Pat grumbled to Katherine Hodge:

'He can call me anything he likes, but somebody's got to write this picture. I'd go to Jack Berners and tell him – but I think we'd both be out on our ears.'

For two days more he camped in René's office, trying to rouse him to action, but with no avail. Desperate on the following day – when the playwright did not even come to the studio – Pat took a benzedrine tablet and attacked the story alone. Pacing his office with the treatment in his hand he dictated to Katherine – interspersing the dictation with a short, biased history of his life in Hollywood. At the day's end he had two pages of script.

The ensuing week was the toughest in his life – not even a moment to make a pass at Katherine Hodge. Gradually, with many creaks, his battered hulk got in motion. Benzedrine and great drafts of coffee woke him in the morning, whiskey anesthetized him at night. Into his feet crept an old neuritis and as his nerves began to crackle he developed a hatred against René Wilcox, which served him as a sort of *ersatz* fuel. He was going to finish the script by himself and hand it to Berners with the statement that Wilcox had not contributed a single line.

But it was too much – Pat was too far gone. He blew up when he was half through and went on a twenty-four-hour bat – and next morning arrived back at the studio to find a message that Mr Berners wanted to see the script at four. Pat was in a sick and confused state when his door opened and René Wilcox came in with a typescript in one hand, and a copy of Berners' note in the other.

'It's all right,' said Wilcox, 'I've finished it.'

'*What?* Have you been *working*?'

'I always work at night.'

'What've you done? A treatment?'

'No, a shooting script. At first I was held back by personal worries, but once I got started it was very simple. You just get behind the camera and dream.'

Pat stood up aghast.

'But we were supposed to collaborate. Jack'll be wild.'

'I've always worked alone,' said Wilcox gently. 'I'll explain to Berners this afternoon.'

Pat sat in a daze. If Wilcox's script was good – but how

could a first script be good? Wilcox should have fed it to him as he wrote; then they might have *had* something.

Fear started his mind working – he was struck by his first original idea since he had been on the job. He phoned to the script department for Katherine Hodge and when she came over told her what he wanted. Katherine hesitated.

'I just want to *read* it,' Pat said hastily. 'If Wilcox is there you can't take it. of course. But he just might be out.'

He waited nervously. In five minutes she was back with the script.

'It isn't mimeographed or even bound,' she said.

He was at the typewriter, trembling as he picked out a letter with two fingers.

'Can I help?' she asked.

'Find me a plain envelope and a used stamp and some paste.'

Pat sealed the letter himself and then gave directions:

'Listen outside Wilcox's office. If he's in, push it under his door. If he's out get a call boy to deliver it to him, wherever he is. Say it's from the mail room. Then you better go off the lot for the afternoon. So he won't catch on, see?'

As she went out Pat wished he had kept a copy of the note. He was proud of it – there was a ring of factual sincerity in it too often missing from his work.

Dear Mr Wilcox:

I am sorry to tell you your two brothers were killed in action today by a long range Tommy-gun. You are wanted at home in England right away.
John Smythe
The British Consulate, New York

But Pat realized that this was no time for self-applause.

He opened Wilcox's script.

To his vast surprise it was technically proficient – the dissolves, fades, cuts, pans and trucking shots were correctly detailed. This simplified everything. Turning back to the first page he wrote at the top:

BALLET SHOES
First Revise
From Pat Hobby and René Wilcox – presently changing this to read: *From René Wilcox and Pat Hobby.*

Then, working frantically, he made several dozen small changes. He substituted the word 'Scram!' for 'Get out of my sight!', he put 'Behind the eight-ball' instead of 'In trouble', and replaced 'You'll be sorry' with the apt coinage 'Or else!' Then he phoned the script department.

'This is Pat Hobby. I've been working on a script with René Wilcox, and Mr Berners would like to have it mimeographed by half-past three.'

This would give him an hour's start on his unconscious collaborator.

'Is it an emergency?'

'I'll say.'

'We'll have to split it up between several girls.'

Pat continued to improve the script till the call boy arrived. He wanted to put in his war idea but time was short – still, he finally told the call boy to sit down, while he wrote laboriously in pencil on the last page.

CLOSE SHOT: *Boris and Rita*
Rita: *What does anything matter now! I have enlisted as a trained nurse in the war*.
Boris (moved): War purifies and regenerates!
(He puts his arms around her in a wild embrace as the music soars way up and we FADE OUT)

Limp and exhausted by his effort he needed a drink so he left the lot and slipped cautiously into the bar across from the studio where he ordered gin and water.

With the glow, he thought warm thoughts. He had done *almost* what he had been hired to do – though his hand had accidentally fallen upon the dialogue rather than the structure. But how could Berners tell that the structure wasn't Pat's ? Katherine Hodge would say nothing, for fear of implicating herself. They were all guilty but guiltiest of all was René Wilcox for refusing to play the game. Always, according to his lights, Pat had played the game.

He had another drink, bought breath tablets and for awhile amused himself at the nickel machine in the drugstore. Louie, the studio bookie, asked if he was interested in wagers on a bigger scale.

'Not today, Louie.'

'What are they paying you, Pat ?'

'Thousand a week.'

'Not so bad.'

'Oh, a lot of us old timers are coming back,' Pat prophesied. 'In silent days was where you got real training – with directors shooting off the cuff and needing a gag in a split second. Now it's a sis job. They got English teachers working in pictures! What do they know ?'

'How about a little something on "Quaker Girl" ?'

'No,' said Pat. 'This afternoon I got an important angle to work on. I don't want to worry about horses.'

At three-fifteen he returned to his office to find two copies of his script in bright new covers.

BALLET SHOES
from
René Wilcox and Pat Hobby
First Revise

It reassured him to see his name in type. As he waited in Jack Berners' anteroom he almost wished he had reversed the names. With the right director this might be another *It Happened One Night*, and if he got his name on something like that it meant a three or four year gravy ride. But this time he'd save his money – go to Santa Anita only once a week – get himself a girl along the type of Katherine Hodge, who wouldn't expect a mansion in Beverly Hills.

Berners' secretary interrupted his reverie, telling him to go in. As he entered he saw with gratification that a copy of the new script lay on Berners' desk.

'Did you ever – ' asked Berners suddenly ' – go to a psychoanalyst?'

'No,' admitted Pat. 'But I suppose I could get up on it. Is it a new assignment?'

'Not exactly. It's just that I think you've lost your grip. Even larceny requires a certain cunning. I've just talked to Wilcox on the phone.'

'Wilcox must be nuts,' said Pat, aggressively. 'I didn't steal anything from him. His name's on it, isn't it? Two weeks ago I laid out all his structure – every scene. I even wrote one whole scene – at the end about the war.'

'Oh yes, the war,' said Berners as if he was thinking of something else.

'But if you like Wilcox's ending better – '

'Yes, I like his ending better. I never saw a man pick up this work so fast.' He paused. 'Pat, you've told the truth just once since you came in this room – that you didn't steal anything from Wilcox.'

'I certainly did not. I *gave* him stuff.'

But a certain dreariness, a grey *malaise*, crept over him as Berners continued:

'I told you we had three scripts. You used an old one

we discarded a year ago. Wilcox was in when your secretary arrived, and he sent one of them to you. Clever, eh?'

Pat was speechless.

'You see, he and that girl like each other. Seems she typed a play for him this summer.'

'They like each other,' said Pat incredulously. 'Why, he –'

'Hold it, Pat. You've had trouble enough today.'

'He's responsible,' Pat cried. 'He wouldn't collaborate – and all the time –'

' – he was writing a swell script. And he can write his own ticket if we can persuade him to stay here and do another.'

Pat could stand no more. He stood up.

'Anyhow thank you, Jack,' he faltered. 'Call my agent if anything turns up.' Then he bolted suddenly and surprisingly for the door.

Jack Berners signaled on the Dictograph for the President's office.

'Get a chance to read it?' he asked in a tone of eagerness.

'It's swell. Better than you said. Wilcox is with me now.'

'Have you signed him up?'

'I'm going to. Seems he wants to work with Hobby. Here you talk to him.'

Wilcox's rather high voice came over the wire.

'Must have Mike Hobby,' he said. 'Grateful to him. Had a quarrel with a certain young lady just before he came, but today Hobby brought us together. Besides, I want to write a play about him. So give him to me – you fellows don't want him any more.'

Berners picked up his secretary's phone.

'Go after Pat Hobby. He's probably in the bar across the

street. We're putting him on salary again but we'll be sorry.'

He switched off, switched on again.

'Oh! Take him his hat. He forgot his hat.'

Pat Hobby and Orson Welles

'Who's this Welles?' Pat asked of Louie, the studio bookie. 'Every time I pick up a paper they got about this Welles.'

'You know, he's that beard,' explained Louie.

'Sure, I know he's that beard, you couldn't miss that. But what credits's he got? What's he done to draw one hundred and fifty grand a picture?'

What indeed? Had he, like Pat, been in Hollywood over twenty years? Did he have credits that would knock your eye out, extending up to – well, up to five years ago when Pat's credits had begun to be few and far between?

'Listen – they don't last long,' said Louie consolingly, 'We've seen 'em come and we've seen 'em go. Hey, Pat?'

Yes – but meanwhile those who had toiled in the vineyard through the heat of the day were lucky to get a few weeks at three-fifty. Men who had once had wives and Filipinos and swimming pools.

'Maybe it's the beard,' said Louie. 'Maybe you and I should grow a beard. My father had a beard but it never got him off Grand Street.'

The gift of hope had remained with Pat through his misfortunes – and the valuable alloy of his hope was proximity. Above all things one must stick around, one must be there when the glazed, tired mind of the producer grappled with the question 'Who?' So presently Pat wandered out of the drugstore, and crossed the street to the lot that was home.

As he passed through the side entrance an unfamiliar studio policeman stood in his way.

'Everybody in the front entrance now.'

'I'm Hobby, the writer,' Pat said.

The Cossack was unimpressed.

'Got your card?'

'I'm between pictures. But I've got an engagement with Jack Berners.'

'Front gate.'

As he turned away Pat thought savagely: 'Lousy Keystone Cop!' In his mind he shot it out with him. Plunk! the stomach. Plunk! plunk! plunk!

At the main entrance, too, there was a new face.

'Where's Ike?' Pat demanded.

'Ike's gone.'

'Well, it's all right, I'm Pat Hobby. Ike always passes me.'

'That's why he's gone,' said the guardian blandly. 'Who's your business with?'

Pat hesitated. He hated to disturb a producer.

'Call Jack Berners' office,' he said. 'Just speak to his secretary.'

After a minute the man turned from the phone.

'What about?' he said.

'About a picture.'

He waited for an answer.

'She wants to know what picture?'

'To hell with it,' said Pat disgustedly. 'Look – call Louie Griebel. What's all this about?'

'Orders from Mr Kasper,' said the clerk. 'Last week a visitor from Chicago fell in the wind machine – Hello. Mr Louie Griebel?'

'I'll talk to him,' said Pat, taking the phone.

'I can't do nothing, Pat,' mourned Louie. 'I had trouble

getting my boy in this morning. Some twirp from Chicago fell in the wind machine.'

'What's that got to do with me?' demanded Pat vehemently.

He walked, a little faster than his wont, along the studio wall to the point where it joined the back lot. There was a guard there but there were always people passing to and fro and he joined one of the groups. Once inside he would see Jack and have himself excepted from this absurd ban. Why, he had known this lot when the first shacks were rising on it, when this was considered the edge of the desert.

'Sorry mister, you with this party?'

'I'm in a hurry,' said Pat. 'I've lost my card.'

'Yeah? Well, for all I know you may be a plain clothes man.' He held open a copy of a photo magazine under Pat's nose, 'I wouldn't let you in even if you told me you was this here Orson Welles.'

II

There is an old Chaplin picture about a crowded street car where the entrance of one man at the rear forces another out in front. A similar image came into Pat's mind in the ensuing days whenever he thought of Orson Welles. Welles was in; Hobby was out. Never before had the studio been barred to Pat and though Welles was on another lot it seemed as if his large body, pushing in brashly from nowhere, had edged Pat out the gate.

'Now where do you go?' Pat thought. He had worked in the other studios but they were not his. At this studio he never felt unemployed – in recent times of stress he had eaten property food on its stages – half a cold lobster during a scene from *The Divine Miss Carstairs*; he had often slept on the sets and last winter made use of a

Chesterfield overcoat from the costume department. Orson Welles had no business edging him out of this. Orson Welles belonged with the rest of the snobs back in New York.

On the third day he was frantic with gloom. He had sent note after note to Jack Berners and even asked Louie to intercede – now word came that Jack had left town. There were so few friends left. Desolate, he stood in front of the automobile gate with a crowd of staring children, feeling that he had reached the end at last.

A great limousine rolled out, in the back of which Pat recognized the great overstuffed Roman face of Harold Marcus. The car rolled toward the children and, as one of them ran in front of it, slowed down. The old man spoke into the tube and the car halted. He leaned out blinking.

'Is there no policeman here ?' he asked of Pat.

'No, Mr Marcus,' said Pat quickly. 'There should be. I'm Pat Hobby, the writer – could you give me a lift down the street ?'

It was unprecedented – it was an act of desperation but Pat's need was great.

Mr Marcus looked at him closely.

'Oh yes, I remember you,' he said. 'Get in.'

He might possibly have meant get up in front with the chauffeur. Pat compromised by opening one of the little seats. Mr Marcus was one of the most powerful men in the whole picture world. He did not occupy himself with production any longer. He spent most of his time rocking from coast to coast on fast trains, merging and launching, launching and merging, like a much divorced woman.

'Some day those children'll get hurt.'

'Yes, Mr Marcus,' agreed Pat heartily. 'Mr Marcus –'

'They ought to have a policeman there.'

'Yes, Mr Marcus. Mr Marcus –'

'Hm-m-m!' said Mr Marcus. 'Where do you want to be dropped?'

Pat geared himself to work fast.

'Mr Marcus, when I was your press agent –'

'I know,' said Mr Marcus. 'You wanted a ten dollar a week raise.'

'What a memory!' cried Pat in gladness. 'What a memory! But Mr Marcus, now I don't want anything at all.'

'This is a miracle.'

'I've got modest wants, see, and I've saved enough to retire.'

He thrust his shoes slightly forward under a hanging blanket. The Chesterfield coat effectively concealed the rest.

'That's what I'd like,' said Mr Marcus gloomily. 'A farm – with chickens. Maybe a little nine-hole course. Not even a stock ticker.'

'I want to retire, but different,' said Pat earnestly. 'Pictures have been my life. I want to watch them grow and grow –'

Mr Marcus groaned.

'Till they explode,' he said. 'Look at Fox! I cried for him.' He pointed to his eyes, 'Tears!'

Pat nodded very sympathetically.

'I want only one thing.' From the long familiarity he went into the foreign locution. 'I should go on the lot anytime. From nothing. Only to be there. Should bother nobody. Only help a little from nothing if any young person wants advice.'

'See Berners,' said Marcus.

'He said see you.'

'Then you did want something,' Marcus smiled. 'All right, all right by me. Where do you get off now?'

'Could you write me a pass?' Pat pleaded. 'Just a word on your card?'

'I'll look into it,' said Mr Marcus. 'Just now I've got things on my mind. I'm going to a luncheon.' He sighed profoundly. 'They want I should meet this new Orson Welles that's in Hollywood.'

Pat's heart winced. There it was again – that name, sinister and remorseless, spreading like a dark cloud over all his skies.

'Mr Marcus,' he said so sincerely that his voice trembled, 'I wouldn't be surprised if Orson Welles is the biggest menace that's come to Hollywood for years. He gets a hundred and fifty grand a picture and I wouldn't be surprised if he was so radical that you had to have all new equipment and start all over again like you did with sound in 1928.'

'Oh my God!' groaned Mr Marcus.

'And me,' said Pat, 'all I want is a pass and no money – to leave things as they are.'

Mr Marcus reached for his card case.

III

To those grouped together under the name 'talent', the atmosphere of a studio is not unfailingly bright – one fluctuates too quickly between high hope and grave apprehension. Those few who decide things are happy in their work and sure that they are worthy of their hire – the rest live in a mist of doubt as to when their vast inadequacy will be disclosed.

Pat's psychology was, oddly, that of the masters and for the most part he was unworried even though he was off salary. But there was one large fly in the ointment – for the first time in his life he began to feel a loss of identity. Due to reasons that he did not quite understand, though it might have been traced to his conversation, a number of people began to address him as 'Orson'.

Now to lose one's identity is a careless thing in any case. But to lose it to an enemy, or at least to one who has become scapegoat for our misfortunes – that is a hardship. Pat was *not* Orson. Any resemblance must be faint and far-fetched and he was aware of the fact. The final effect was to make him, in that regard, something of an eccentric.

'Pat,' said Joe the barber, 'Orson was in here today and asked me to trim his beard.'

'I hope you set fire to it,' said Pat.

'I did,' Joe winked at waiting customers over a hot towel. 'He asked for a singe so I took it all off. Now his face is as bald as yours. In fact you look a bit alike.'

This was the morning the kidding was so ubiquitous that, to avoid it, Pat lingered in Mario's bar across the street. He was not drinking – at the bar, that is, for he was down to his last thirty cents, but he refreshed himself frequently from a half-pint in his back pocket. He needed the stimulus for he had to make a touch presently and he knew that money was easier to borrow when one didn't have an air of urgent need.

His quarry, Jeff Boldini, was in an unsympathetic state of mind. He too was an artist, albeit a successful one, and a certain great lady of the screen had just burned him up by criticizing a wig he had made for her. He told the story to Pat at length and the latter waited until it was all out before broaching his request.

'No soap,' said Jeff. 'Hell, you never paid me back what you borrowed last month.'

'But I got a job now,' lied Pat. 'This is just to tide me over. I start tomorrow.'

'If they don't give the job to Orson Welles,' said Jeff humorously.

Pat's eyes narrowed but he managed to utter a polite, borrower's laugh.

'Hold it,' said Jeff. 'You know I think you look like him?'

'Yeah.'

'Honest. Anyhow I could make you look like him. I could make you a beard that would be his double.'

'I wouldn't be his double for fifty grand.'

With his head on one side Jeff regarded Pat.

'I could,' he said. 'Come on in to my chair and let me see.'

'Like hell.'

'Come on. I'd like to try it. You haven't got anything to do. You don't work till tomorrow.'

'I don't want a beard.'

'It'll come off.'

'I don't want it.'

'It won't cost you anything. In fact I'll be paying *you* – I'll loan you the ten smackers if you'll let me make you a beard.'

Half an hour later Jeff looked at his completed work.

'It's perfect,' he said. 'Not only the beard but the eyes and everything.'

'All right. Now take it off,' said Pat moodily.

'What's the hurry? That's a fine muff. That's a work of art. We ought to put a camera on it. Too bad you're working tomorrow – they're using a dozen beards out on Sam Jones' set and one of them went to jail in a homo raid. I bet with that muff you could get the job.'

It was weeks since Pat had heard the word job and he could not himself say how he managed to exist and eat. Jeff saw the light in his eye.

'What say? Let me drive you out there just for fun,' pleaded Jeff. 'I'd like to see if Sam could tell it was a phony muff.'

'I'm a writer, not a ham.'

'Come on! Nobody would never know you back of that. And you'd draw another ten bucks.'

As they left the make-up department Jeff lingered behind a minute. On a strip of cardboard he crayoned the name Orson Welles in large block letters. And outside without Pat's notice, he stuck it in the windshield of his car.

He did not go directly to the back lot. Instead he drove not too swiftly up the main studio street. In front of the administration building he stopped on the pretext that the engine was missing, and almost in no time a small but definitely interested crowd began to gather. But Jeff's plans did not include stopping anywhere long, so he hopped in and they started on a tour around the commissary.

'Where are we going?' demanded Pat.

He had already made one nervous attempt to tear the beard from him, but to his surprise it did not come away.

He complained of this to Jeff.

'Sure,' Jeff explained. 'That's made to last. You'll have to soak it off.'

The car paused momentarily at the door of the commissary. Pat saw blank eyes staring at him and he stared back at them blankly from the rear seat.

'You'd think I was the only beard on the lot,' he said gloomily.

'You can sympathize with Orson Welles.'

'To hell with him.'

This colloquy would have puzzled those without, to whom he was nothing less than the real McCoy.

Jeff drove on slowly up the street. Ahead of them a little group of men were walking – one of them, turning, saw the car and drew the attention of the others to it. Whereupon the most elderly member of the party threw up his arms in what appeared to be a defensive gesture, and plunged to the sidewalk as the car went past.

'My God, did you see that?' exclaimed Jeff. 'That was Mr Marcus.'

He came to a stop. An excited man ran up and put his head in the car window.

'Mr Welles, our Mr Marcus has had a heart attack. Can we use your car to get him to the infirmary?'

Pat stared. Then very quickly he opened the door on the other side and dashed from the car. Not even the beard could impede his streamlined flight. The policeman at the gate, not recognizing the incarnation, tried to have words with him but Pat shook him off with the ease of a triple-threat back and never paused till he reached Mario's bar.

Three extras with beards stood at the rail, and with relief Pat merged himself into their corporate whiskers. With a trembling hand he took the hard-earned ten dollar bill from his pocket.

'Set 'em up,' he cried hoarsely. 'Every muff has a drink on me.'

Pat Hobby's Secret

Distress in Hollywood is endemic and always acute. Scarcely an executive but is being gnawed at by some insoluble problem and in a democratic way he will let you in on it, with no charge. The problem, be it one of health or of production, is faced courageously and with groans at from one to five thousand a week. That's how pictures are made.

'But this one has got me down,' said Mr Banizon, ' – because how did the artillery shell get in the trunk of Claudette Colbert or Betty Field or whoever we decide to use? We got to explain it so the audience will believe it.'

He was in the office of Louie the studio bookie and his present audience also included Pat Hobby, venerable script-stooge of forty-nine. Mr Banizon did not expect a suggestion from either of them but he had been talking aloud to himself about the problem for a week now and was unable to stop.

'Who's your writer on it?' asked Louie.

'R. Parke Woll,' said Banizon indignantly. 'First I buy this opening from another writer, see. A grand notion but only a notion. Then I call in R. Parke Woll, the playwright, and we meet a couple of times and develop it. Then when we get the end in sight, his agent horns in and says he won't let Woll talk any more unless I give him a contract – eight weeks at $3,000! And all I need him for is one more day!'

The sum brought a glitter into Pat's old eyes. Ten years

ago he had camped beatifically in range of such a salary –
now he was lucky to get a few weeks at $250. His inflamed
and burnt over talent had failed to produce a second
growth.

'The worse part of it is that Woll told me the ending,'
continued the producer.

'Then what are you waiting for?' demanded Pat. 'You
don't need to pay him a cent.'

'I forgot it!' groaned Mr Banizon. 'Two phones were
ringing at once in my office – one from a working director.
And while I was talking Woll had to run along. Now I can't
remember it and I can't get him back.'

Perversely Pat Hobby's sense of justice was with the
producer, not the writer. Banizon had almost outsmarted
Woll and then been cheated by a tough break. And now
the playwright, with the insolence of an Eastern snob, was
holding him up for twenty-four grand. What with the
European market gone. What with the war.

'Now he's on a big bat,' said Banizon. 'I know because
I got a man tailing him. It's enough to drive you nuts –
here I got the whole story except the pay-off. What good
is it to me like that?'

'If he's drunk maybe he'd spill it,' suggested Louie prac-
tically.

'Not to me,' said Mr Banizon. 'I thought of it but he
would recognize my face.'

Having reached the end of his current blind alley, Mr
Banizon picked a horse in the third and one in the seventh
and prepared to depart.

'I got an idea,' said Pat.

Mr Banizon looked suspiciously at the red old eyes.

'I got no time to hear it now,' he said.

'I'm not selling anything,' Pat reassured him. 'I got a
deal almost ready over at Paramount. But once I worked

with this R. Parke Woll and maybe I could find what you want to know.'

He and Mr Banizon went out of the office together and walked slowly across the lot. An hour later, for an advance consideration of fifty dollars, Pat was employed to discover how a live artillery shell got into Claudette Colbert's trunk or Betty Field's trunk or whosoever's trunk it should be.

II

The swath which R. Parke Woll was now cutting through the City of the Angels would have attracted no special notice in the twenties; in the fearful forties it rang out like laughter in church. He was easy to follow: his absence had been requested from two hotels but he had settled down into a routine where he carried his sleeping quarters in his elbow. A small but alert band of rats and weasels were furnishing him moral support in his journey – a journey which Pat caught up with at two a.m. in Conk's Old Fashioned Bar.

Conk's Bar was haughtier than its name, boasting cigarette girls and a doorman-bouncer named Smith who had once stayed a full hour with Tarzan White. Mr Smith was an embittered man who expressed himself by goosing the patrons on their way in and out and this was Pat's introduction. When he recovered himself he discovered R. Parke Woll in a mixed company around a table, and sauntered up with an air of surprise.

'Hello, good looking,' he said to Woll. 'Remember me – Pat Hobby?'

R. Parke Woll brought him with difficulty into focus, turning his head first on one side then on the other, letting it sink, snap up and then lash forward like a cobra taking a candid snapshot. Evidently it recorded for he said:

'Pat Hobby! Sit down and wha'll you have. Genlemen, this is Pat Hobby – best left-handed writer in Hollywood. Pat h'are you?'

Pat sat down, amid suspicious looks from a dozen predatory eyes. Was Pat an old friend sent to get the playwright home?

Pat saw this and waited until a half-hour later when he found himself alone with Woll in the washroom.

'Listen Parke, Banizon is having you followed,' he said. 'I don't know why he's doing it. Louie at the studio tipped me off.'

'You don't know why?' cried Parke. 'Well, I know why. I got something he wants – that's why!'

'You owe him money?'

'Owe him money. Why that – he owes *me* money! He owes me for three long, hard conferences – I outlined a whole damn picture for him.' His vague finger tapped his forehead in several places. 'What he wants is in here.'

An hour passed at the turbulent orgiastic table. Pat waited – and then inevitably in the slow, limited cycle of the lush, Woll's mind returned to the subject.

'The funny thing is I told him who put the shell in the trunk and why. And then the Master Mind forgot.'

Pat had an inspiration.

'But his secretary remembered.'

'She did?' Woll was flabbergasted. 'Secretary – don't remember secretary.'

'She came in,' ventured Pat uneasily.

'Well then by God he's got to pay me or I'll sue him.'

'Banizon says he's got a better idea.'

'The hell he has. My idea was a pip. Listen – '

He spoke for two minutes.

'You like it?' he demanded. He looked at Pat for applause – then he must have seen something in Pat's eye that he was not intended to see. 'Why you little skunk,' he cried. 'You've talked to Banizon – he sent you here.'

Pat rose and tore like a rabbit for the door. He would have been out into the street before Woll could overtake him had it not been for the intervention of Mr Smith, the doorman.

'Where you going?' he demanded, catching Pat by his lapels.

'Hold him!' cried Woll, coming up. He aimed a blow at Pat which missed and landed full in Mr Smith's mouth.

It has been mentioned that Mr Smith was an embittered as well as a powerful man. He dropped Pat, picked up R. Parke Woll by crotch and shoulder, held him high and then in one gigantic pound brought his body down against the floor. Three minutes later Woll was dead.

III

Except in great scandals like the Arbuckle case the industry protects its own – and the industry included Pat, however intermittently. He was let out of prison next morning without bail, wanted only as a material witness. If anything, the publicity was advantageous – for the first time in a year his name appeared in the trade journals. Moreover he was now the only living man who knew how the shell got into Claudette Colbert's (or Betty Field's) trunk.

'When can you come up and see me?' said Mr Banizon.

'After the inquest tomorrow,' said Pat enjoying himself. 'I feel kind of shaken – it gave me an earache.'

That too indicated power. Only those who were 'in' could speak of their health and be listened to.

'Woll really did tell you?' questioned Banizon.

'He told me,' said Pat. 'And it's worth more than fifty

smackers. I'm going to get me a new agent and bring him to your office.'

'I tell you a better plan,' said Banizon hastily, 'I'll get you on the payroll. Four weeks at your regular price.'

'What's my price?' demanded Pat gloomily. 'I've drawn everything from four thousand to zero.' And he added ambiguously, 'As Shakespeare says, "Every man has his price."'

The attendant rodents of R. Parke Woll had vanished with their small plunger into convenient rat holes, leaving as the defendant Mr Smith, and, as witnesses, Pat and two frightened cigarette girls. Mr Smith's defense was that he had been attacked. At the inquest one cigarette girl agreed with him – one condemned him for unnecessary roughness. Pat Hobby's turn was next, but before his name was called he started as a voice spoke to him from behind.

'You talk against my husband and I'll twist your tongue out by the roots.'

A huge dinosaur of a woman, fully six feet tall and broad in proportion, was leaning forward against his chair.

'Pat Hobby, step forward please ... now Mr Hobby tell us exactly what happened.'

The eyes of Mr Smith were fixed balefully on his and he felt the eyes of the bouncer's mate reaching in for his tongue through the back of his head. He was full of natural hesitation.

'I don't know exactly,' he said, and then with quick inspiration, 'All I know is everything went white!'

'*What?*'

'That's the way it was. I saw white. Just like some guys see red or black I saw white.'

There was some consultation among the authorities.

'Well, what happened from when you came into the restaurant – up to the time you saw white?'

'Well – ' said Pat fighting for time. 'It was all kind of that way. I came and sat down and then it began to go black.'

'You mean white.'

'Black *and* white.'

There was a general titter.

'Witness dismissed. Defendant remanded for trial.'

What was a little joking to endure when the stakes were so high – all that night a mountainous Amazon pursued him through his dreams and he needed a strong drink before appearing at Mr Banizon's office next morning. He was accompanied by one of the few Hollywood agents who had not yet taken him on and shaken him off.

'A flat sum of five hundred,' offered Banizon. 'Or four weeks at two-fifty to work on another picture.'

'How bad do you want this?' asked the agent. 'My client seems to think it's worth three thousand.'

'Of my own money?' cried Banizon. 'And it isn't even *his* idea. Now that Woll is dead it's in the Public Remains.'

'Not quite,' said the agent. 'I think like you do that ideas are sort of in the air. They belong to whoever's got them at the time – like balloons.'

'Well, how much?' asked Mr Banizon fearfully. 'How do I know he's got the idea?'

The agent turned to Pat.

'Shall we let him find out – for a thousand dollars?'

After a moment Pat nodded. Something was bothering him.

'All right,' said Banizon. 'This strain is driving me nuts. One thousand.'

There was silence.

'Spill it Pat,' said the agent.

Still no word from Pat. They waited. When Pat spoke at last his voice seemed to come from afar.

'Everything's white,' he gasped.

'*What?*'

'I can't help it – everything has gone white. I can see it – white. I remember going into the joint but after that it all goes white.'

For a moment they thought he was holding out. Then the agent realized that Pat actually had drawn a psychological blank. The secret of R. Parke Woll was safe forever.

Too late Pat realized that a thousand dollars was slipping away and tried desperately to recover.

'I remember, I remember! It was put in by some Nazi dictator.'

'Maybe the girl put it in the trunk herself,' said Banizon ironically. 'For her bracelet.'

For many years Mr Banizon would be somewhat gnawed by this insoluble problem. And as he glowered at Pat he wished that writers could be dispensed with altogether. If only ideas could be plucked from the inexpensive air!

Pat Hobby, Putative Father

Most writers look like writers whether they want to or not. It is hard to say why – for they model their exteriors whimsically on Wall Street brokers, cattle kings or English explorers – but they all turn out looking like writers, as definitely typed as 'The Public' or 'The Profiteers' in the cartoons.

Pat Hobby was the exception. He did not look like a writer. And only in one corner of the Republic could he have **been** identified as a member of the entertainment world. Even there the first guess would have been that he was an extra down on his luck, or a bit player who specialized in the sort of father who should *never* come home. But a writer he was: he had collaborated in over two dozen moving picture scripts, most of them, it must be admitted, prior to 1929.

A writer? He had a desk in the Writers' Building at the studio; he had pencils, paper, a secretary, paper clips, a pad for office memoranda. And he sat in an overstuffed chair, his eyes not so very bloodshot, taking in the morning's *Reporter*.

'I got to get to work,' he told Miss Raudenbush at eleven. And again at twelve:

'I got to get to work.'

At quarter to one, he began to feel hungry – up to this point every move, or rather every moment, was in the writer's tradition. Even to the faint irritation that no one had annoyed him, no one had bothered him, no one had interfered with the long empty dream which constituted his average day.

He was about to accuse his secretary of staring at him when the welcome interruption came. A studio guide tapped at his door and brought him a note from his boss, Jack Berners:

Dear Pat:
   Please take some time off and show these people around the lot.

                                                            Jack

'My God!' Pat exclaimed. 'How can I be expected to get anything done and show people around the lot at the same time. Who are they?' he demanded of the guide.

'I don't know. One of them seems to be kind of colored. He looks like the extras they had at Paramount for *Bengal Lancer*. He can't speak English. The other –'

Pat was putting on his coat to see for himself.

'Will you be wanting me this afternoon?' asked Miss Raudenbush.

He looked at her with infinite reproach and went out in front of the Writers' Building.

The visitors were there. The sultry person was tall and of a fine carriage, dressed in excellent English clothes except for a turban. The other was a youth of fifteen, quite light of hue. He also wore a turban with beautifully cut jodhpurs and riding coat.

They bowed formally.

'Hear you want to go on some sets,' said Pat. 'You friends of Jack Berners?'

'Acquaintances,' said the youth. 'May I present you to my uncle: Sir Singrim Dak Raj.'

Probably, thought Pat, the company was cooking up a Bengal Lancers, and this man would play the heavy who owned the Khyber Pass. Maybe they'd put Pat on it – at three-fifty a week. Why not? He knew how to write that stuff:

Beautiful Long Shot. The Gorge. Show Tribesman firing from behind rocks.

Medium Shot. Tribesman hit by bullet making nose dive over high rock. (use stunt man)

Medium Long Shot. The Valley. British troops wheeling out cannon.

'You going to be long in Hollywood?' he asked shrewdly.

'My uncle doesn't speak English,' said the youth in a measured voice. 'We are here only a few days. You see – I am your putative son.'

II

' – And I would very much like to see Bonita Granville,' continued the youth. 'I find she has been borrowed by your studio.'

They had been walking toward the production office and it took Pat a minute to grasp what the young man had said.

'You're my what?' he asked.

'Your putative son,' said the young man, in a sort of sing-song. 'Legally I am the son and heir of the Rajah Dak Raj Indore. But I was born John Brown Hobby.'

'Yes?' said Pat. 'Go on! What's this?'

'My mother was Delia Brown. You married her in 1926. And she divorced you in 1927 when I was a few months old. Later she took me to India, where she married my present legal father.'

'Oh,' said Pat. They had reached the production office. 'You want to see Bonita Granville.'

'Yes,' said John Hobby Indore. 'If it is convenient.'

Pat looked at the shooting schedule on the wall.

'It may be,' he said heavily. 'We can go and see.'

As they started toward Stage 4, he exploded.

'What do you mean, "my potato son"? I'm glad to see you and all that, but say, are you really the kid Delia had in 1926?'

'Putatively,' John Indore said. 'At that time you and she were legally married.'

He turned to his uncle and spoke rapidly in Hindustani, whereupon the latter bent forward, looked with cold examination upon Pat and threw up his shoulders without comment. The whole business was making Pat vaguely uncomfortable.

When he pointed out the commissary, John wanted to stop there 'to buy his uncle a hot dog'. It seemed that Sir Singrim had conceived a passion for them at the World's Fair in New York, whence they had just come. They were taking ship for Madras tomorrow.

' – whether or not,' said John, somberly, 'I get to see Bonita Granville. I do not care if I *meet* her. I am too young for her. She is already an old woman by our standards. But I'd like to *see* her.'

It was one of those bad days for showing people around. Only one of the directors shooting today was an old timer, on whom Pat could count for a welcome – and at the door of that stage he received word that the star kept blowing up in his lines and had demanded that the set be cleared.

In desperation he took his charges out to the back lot and walked them past the false fronts of ships and cities and village streets, and medieval gates – a sight in which the boy showed a certain interest but which Sir Singrim found disappointing. Each time that Pat led them around behind to demonstrate that it was all phony Sir Singrim's expression would change to disappointment and faint contempt.

'What's he say?' Pat asked his offspring, after Sir Singrim had walked eagerly into a Fifth Avenue jewelry store, to find nothing but carpenter's rubble inside.

'He is the third richest man in India,' said John. 'He is disgusted. He says he will never enjoy an American picture again. He says he will buy one of our picture companies in India and make every set as solid as the Taj Mahal. He thinks perhaps the actresses just have a false front too, and that's why you won't let us see them.'

The first sentence had rung a sort of carillon in Pat's head. If there was anything he liked it was a good piece of money – not this miserable, uncertain two-fifty a week which purchased his freedom.

'I'll tell you,' he said with sudden decision. 'We'll try Stage 4, and peek at Bonita Granville.'

Stage 4 was double locked and barred, for the day – the director hated visitors, and it was a process stage besides. 'Process' was a generic name for trick photography in which every studio competed with other studios, and lived in terror of spies. More specifically it meant that a projecting machine threw a moving background upon a transparent screen. On the other side of the screen, a scene was played and recorded against this moving background. The projector on one side of the screen and the camera on the other were so synchronized that the result could show a star standing on his head before an indifferent crowd on 42nd Street – a *real* crowd and a *real* star – and the poor eye could only conclude that it was being deluded and never quite guess how.

Pat tried to explain this to John, but John was peering for Bonita Granville from behind the great mass of coiled ropes and pails where they hid. They had not got there by the front entrance, but by a little side door for technicians that Pat knew.

Wearied by the long jaunt over the back lot, Pat took a pint flask from his hip and offered it to Sir Singrim who declined. He did not offer it to John.

'Stunt your growth,' he said solemnly, taking a long pull.

'I do not want any,' said John with dignity.

He was suddenly alert. He had spotted an idol more glamorous than Siva not twenty feet away – her back, her profile, her voice. Then she moved off.

Watching his face, Pat was rather touched.

'We can go nearer,' he said. 'We might get to that ball-room set. They're not using it – they got covers on the furniture.'

On tip toe they started, Pat in the lead, then Sir Singrim, then John. As they moved softly forward Pat heard the words 'Lights' and stopped in his tracks. Then, as a blinding white glow struck at their eyes and the voice shouted 'Quiet! We're rolling!' Pat began to run, followed quickly through the white silence by the others.

The silence did not endure.

'*Cut!*' screamed a voice, 'What the living, blazing hell!'

From the director's angle something had happened on the screen which, for the moment, was inexplicable. Three gigantic silhouettes, two with huge Indian turbans, had danced across what was intended to be a New England Harbor – they had blundered into the line of the process shot. Prince John Indore had not only seen Bonita Granville – he had acted in the same picture. His silhouetted foot seemed to pass miraculously through her blonde young head.

II

They sat for some time in the guard-room before word could be gotten to Jack Berners, who was off the lot. So there was leisure for talk. This consisted of a longish harangue from Sir Singrim to John, which the latter – modifying its tone if not its words – translated to Pat.

'My uncle says his brother wanted to do something for you. He thought perhaps if you were a great writer he might invite you to come to his kingdom and write his life.'

'I never claimed to be – '

'My uncle says you are an ignominous writer – in your own land you permitted him to be touched by those dogs of the policemen.'

'Aw – bananas,' muttered Pat uncomfortably.

'He says my mother always wished you well. But now she is a high and sacred lady and should never see you again. He says we will go to our chambers in the Ambassador Hotel and meditate and pray and let you know what we decide.'

When they were released, and the two moguls were escorted apologetically to their car by a studio yes-man, it seemed to Pat that it had been pretty well decided already. He was angry. For the sake of getting his son a peek at Miss Granville, he had quite possibly lost his job – though he didn't really think so. Or rather he was pretty sure that when his week was up he would have lost it anyhow. But though it was a pretty bad break he remembered most clearly from the afternoon that Sir Singrim was 'the third richest man in India', and after dinner at a bar on La Cienega he decided to go down to the Ambassador Hotel and find out the result of the prayer and meditation.

It was early dark of a September evening. The Ambassador was full of memories to Pat – the Coconut Grove in the great days, when directors found pretty girls in the afternoon and made stars of them by night. There was some activity in front of the door and Pat watched it idly.

Such a quantity of baggage he had seldom seen, even in the train of Gloria Swanson or Joan Crawford. Then he started as he saw two or three men in turbans moving around among the baggage. So – they were running out on him.

Sir Singrim Dak Raj and his nephew Prince John, both pulling on gloves as if at a command, appeared at the door, as Pat stepped forward out of the darkness.

'Taking a powder, eh?' he said. 'Say when you get back there, tell them that one American could lick – '

'I have left a note for you,' said Prince John, turning from his Uncle's side. 'I say, you *were* nice this afternoon and it really was too bad.'

'Yes, it was,' agreed Pat.

'But we are providing for you,' John said. 'After our prayers we decided that you will receive fifty sovereigns a month – two hundred and fifty dollars – for the rest of your natural life.'

'What will I have to do for it?' questioned Pat suspiciously.

'It will only be withdrawn in case – '

John leaned and whispered in Pat's ear, and relief crept into Pat's eyes. The condition had nothing to do with drink and blondes, really nothing to do with him at all.

John began to get in the limousine.

'Goodbye, putative father,' he said, almost with affection.

Pat stood looking after him.

'Goodbye son,' he said. He stood watching the limousine go out of sight. Then he turned away – feeling like – like Stella Dallas. There were tears in his eyes.

Potato Father – whatever that meant. After some consideration he added to himself: it's better than not being a father at all.

IV

He awoke late next afternoon with a happy hangover – the cause of which he could not determine until young John's voice seemed to spring into his ears, repeating: 'Fifty sovereigns a month, with just one condition – that it be withdrawn in case of war, when all revenues of our state will revert to the British Empire.'

With a cry Pat sprang to the door. No *Los Angeles Times* lay against it, no *Examiner* – only *Toddy's Daily Form Sheet*. He searched the orange pages frantically. Below the form sheets, the past performances, the endless oracles for endless racetracks, his eye was caught by a one-inch item:

LONDON, SEPTEMBER 3RD. ON THIS MORNING'S DECLARATION BY CHAMBERLAIN, DOUGIE CABLES 'ENGLAND TO WIN, FRANCE TO PLACE, RUSSIA TO SHOW'.

The Homes of the Stars

Beneath a great striped umbrella at the side of a boulevard in a Hollywood heat wave, sat a man. His name was Gus Venske (no relation to the runner) and he wore magenta pants, cerise shoes and a sport article from Vine Street which resembled nothing so much as a cerulean blue pajama top.

Gus Venske was not a freak nor were his clothes at all extraordinary for his time and place. He had a profession – on a pole beside the umbrella was a placard:

VISIT THE HOMES OF THE STARS

Business was bad or Gus would not have hailed the unprosperous man who stood in the street beside a panting, steaming car, anxiously watching its efforts to cool.

'Hey fella,' said Gus, without much hope. 'Wanna visit the homes of the stars?'

The red-rimmed eyes of the watcher turned from the automobile and looked superciliously upon Gus.

'I'm *in* pictures,' said the man, 'I'm in 'em myself.'

'Actor?'

'No. Writer.'

Pat Hobby turned back to his car, which was whistling like a peanut wagon. He had told the truth – or what was once the truth. Often in the old days his name had flashed on the screen for the few seconds allotted to authorship, but for the past five years his services had been less and less in demand.

Presently Gus Venske shut up shop for lunch by putting his folders and maps into a briefcase and walking off with it under his arm. As the sun grew hotter moment by moment, Pat Hobby took refuge under the faint protection of the umbrella and inspected a soiled folder which had been dropped by Mr Venske. If Pat had not been down to his last fourteen cents he would have telephoned a garage for aid – as it was, he could only wait.

After a while a limousine with a Missouri license drew to rest beside him. Behind the chauffeur sat a little white moustached man and a large woman with a small dog. They conversed for a moment – then, in a rather shame-faced way, the woman leaned out and addressed Pat.

'What stars' homes can you visit ?' she asked.

It took a moment for this to sink in.

'I mean can we go to Robert Taylor's home and Clark Gable's and Shirley Temple's – '

'I guess you can if you can get in,' said Pat.

'Because – ' continued the woman, ' – if we could go to the very best homes, the most exclusive – we would be prepared to pay more than your regular price.'

Light dawned upon Pat. Here together were suckers and smackers. Here was that dearest of Hollywood dreams – the angle. If one got the right angle it meant meals at the Brown Derby, long nights with bottles and girls, a new tire for his old car. And here was an angle fairly thrusting itself at him.

He rose and went to the side of the limousine.

'Sure. Maybe I could fix it.' As he spoke he felt a pang of doubt. 'Would you be able to pay in advance ?'

The couple exchanged a look.

'Suppose we gave you five dollars now,' the woman said, 'and five dollars if we can visit Clark Gable's home or somebody like that.'

Once upon a time such a thing would have been so easy. In his salad days when Pat had twelve or fifteen writing credits a year, he could have called up many people who would have said, 'Sure, Pat, if it means anything to you.' But now he could only think of a handful who really recognized him and spoke to him around the lots – Melvyn Douglas and Robert Young and Ronald Colman and Young Doug. Those he had known best had retired or passed away.

And he did not know except vaguely where the new stars lived, but he had noticed that on the folder were type-written several dozen names and addresses with penciled checks after each.

'Of course you can't be sure anybody's at home,' he said, 'they might be working in the studios.'

'We understand that.' The lady glanced at Pat's car, glanced away. 'We'd better go in our motor.'

'Sure.'

Pat got up in front with the chauffeur – trying to think fast. The actor who spoke to him most pleasantly was Ronald Colman – they had never exchanged more than conventional salutations but he might pretend that he was calling to interest Colman in a story.

Better still, Colman was probably not at home and Pat might wangle his clients an inside glimpse of the house. Then the process might be repeated at Robert Young's house and Young Doug's and Melvyn Douglas'. By that time the lady would have forgotten Gable and the afternoon would be over.

He looked at Ronald Colman's address on the folder and gave the direction to the chauffeur.

'We know a woman who had her picture taken with George Brent,' said the lady as they started off, 'Mrs Horace J. Ives, Jr.'

'She's our neighbor,' said her husband. 'She lives at 372 Rose Drive in Kansas City. And we live at 327.'

'She had her picture taken with George Brent. We always wondered if she had to pay for it. Of course I don't know that I'd want to go so far as *that*. I don't know what they'd say back home.'

'I don't think we want to go as far as all that,' agreed her husband.

'Where are we going first?' asked the lady, cosily.

'Well, I had a couple calls to pay anyhow,' said Pat. 'I got to see Ronald Colman about something.'

'Oh, he's one of my favorites. Do you know him well?'

'Oh yes,' said Pat, 'I'm not in this business regularly. I'm just doing it today for a friend. I'm a writer.'

Sure in the knowledge that not so much as a trio of picture writers were known to the public he named himself as the author of several recent successes.

'That's very interesting,' said the man, 'I knew a writer once – this Upton Sinclair or Sinclair Lewis. Not a bad fellow even if he was a socialist.'

'Why aren't you writing a picture now?' asked the lady.

'Well, you see we're on strike,' Pat invented. 'We got a thing called the Screen Playwriters' Guild and we're on strike.'

'Oh.' His clients stared with suspicion at this emissary of Stalin in the front seat of their car.

'What are you striking for?' asked the man uneasily.

Pat's political development was rudimentary. He hesitated.

'Oh, better living conditions,' he said finally, 'free pencils and paper. I don't know – it's all in the Wagner Act.' After a moment he added vaguely, 'Recognize Finland.'

'I didn't know writers had unions,' said the man. 'Well, if you're on strike who writes the movies?'

'The producers,' said Pat bitterly. 'That's why they're so lousy.'

'Well, that's what I would call an odd state of things.'

They came in sight of Ronald Colman's house and Pat swallowed uneasily. A shining new roadster sat out in front.

'I better go in first,' he said. 'I mean we wouldn't want to come in on any – on any family scene or anything.'

'Does he have family scenes?' asked the lady eagerly.

'Oh, well, you know how people are,' said Pat with charity. 'I think I ought to see how things are first.'

The car stopped. Drawing a long breath Pat got out. At the same moment the door of the house opened and Ronald Colman hurried down the walk. Pat's heart missed a beat as the actor glanced in his direction.

'Hello Pat,' he said. Evidently he had no notion that Pat was a caller for he jumped into his car and the sound of his motor drowned out Pat's responses as he drove away.

'Well, he called you "Pat",' said the woman impressed.

'I guess he was in a hurry,' said Pat. 'But maybe we could see his house.'

He rehearsed a speech going up the walk. He had just spoken to his friend Mr Colman, and received permission to look around.

But the house was shut and locked and there was no answer to the bell. He would have to try Melvyn Douglas whose salutations, on second thought, were a little warmer than Ronald Colman's. At any rate his clients' faith in him was now firmly founded. The 'Hello, Pat,' rang confidently in their ears; by proxy they were already inside the charmed circle.

'Now let's try Clark Gable's,' said the lady. 'I'd like to tell Carole Lombard about her hair.'

The lese majesty made Pat's stomach wince. Once in a

crowd he had met Clark Gable but he had no reason to believe that Mr Gable remembered.

'Well, we could try Melvyn Douglas' first and then Bob Young or else Young Doug. They're all on the way. You see Gable and Lombard live away out in the St Joaquin valley.'

'Oh,' said the lady disappointed, 'I did want to run up and see their bedroom. Well then, our next choice would be Shirley Temple.' She looked at her little dog. 'I know that would be Boojie's choice too.'

'They're kind of afraid of kidnappers,' said Pat.

Ruffled, the man produced his business card and handed it to Pat.

DEERING R. ROBINSON
Vice President and Chairman
of the Board
Robdeer Food Products

'Does *that* sound as if I want to kidnap Shirley Temple?'

'They just have to be sure,' said Pat apologetically. 'After we go to Melvyn – '

'No – let's see Shirley Temple's *now*,' insisted the woman. 'Really! I told you in the first place what I wanted.'

Pat hesitated.

'First I'll have to stop in some drugstore and phone about it.'

In a drugstore he exchanged some of the five dollars for a half pint of gin and took two long swallows behind a high counter, after which he considered the situation. He could, of course, duck Mr and Mrs Robinson immediately – after all he had produced Ronald Colman, with sound, for their five smackers. On the other hand they just *might* catch Miss Temple on her way in or out – and for a pleasant day at Santa Anita tomorrow Pat needed five smackers more. In the glow of the gin his courage mounted, and returning to the limousine he gave the chauffeur the address.

But approaching the Temple house his spirit quailed as he saw that there was a tall iron fence and an electric gate. And didn't guides have to have a license?

'Not here,' he said quickly to the chauffeur. 'I made a mistake. I think it's the next one, or two or three doors further on.'

He decided on a large mansion set in an open lawn and stopping the chauffeur got out and walked up to the door. He was temporarily licked but at least he might bring back some story to soften them – say, that Miss Temple had mumps. He could point out her sick-room from the walk.

There was no answer to his ring but he saw that the door was partly ajar. Cautiously he pushed it open. He was staring into a deserted living room on the baronial scale. He listened. There was no one about, no footsteps on the upper floor, no murmur from the kitchen. Pat took another pull at the gin. Then swiftly he hurried back to the limousine.

'She's at the studio,' he said quickly. 'But if we're quiet we can look at their living-room.'

Eagerly the Robinsons and Boojie disembarked and followed him. The living-room might have been Shirley Temple's, might have been one of many in Hollywood. Pat saw a doll in a corner and pointed at it, whereupon Mrs Robinson picked it up, looked at it reverently and showed it to Boojie who sniffed indifferently.

'Could I meet Mrs Temple?' she asked.

'Oh, she's out – nobody's home,' Pat said – unwisely.

'Nobody. Oh – then Boojie would so like a wee little peep at her bedroom.'

Before he could answer she had run up the stairs. Mr Robinson followed and Pat waited uneasily in the hall, ready to depart at the sound either of an arrival outside or a commotion above.

He finished the bottle, disposed of it politely under a sofa cushion and then deciding that the visit upstairs was tempting fate too far, he went after his clients. On the stairs he heard Mrs Robinson.

'But there's only *one* child's bedroom. I thought Shirley had brothers.'

A window on the winding staircase looked upon the street, and glancing out Pat saw a large car drive up to the curb. From it stepped a Hollywood celebrity who, though not one of those pursued by Mrs Robinson was second to none in prestige and power. It was old Mr Marcus, the producer, for whom Pat Hobby had been press agent twenty years ago.

At this point Pat lost his head. In a flash he pictured an elaborate explanation as to what he was doing here. He would not be forgiven. His occasional weeks in the studio at two-fifty would now disappear altogether and another finis would be written to his almost entirely finished career. He left, impetuously and swiftly – down the stairs, through the kitchen and out the back gate, leaving the Robinsons to their destiny.

Vaguely he was sorry for them as he walked quickly along the next boulevard. He could see Mr Robinson producing his card as the head of Robdeer Food Products. He could see Mr Marcus' skepticism, the arrival of the police, the frisking of Mr and Mrs Robinson.

Probably it would stop there – except that the Robinsons would be furious at him for his imposition. They would tell the police where they had picked him up.

Suddenly he went ricketing down the street, beads of

gin breaking out profusely on his forehead. He had left his car beside Gus Venske's umbrella. And now he remembered another recognizing clue and hoped that Ronald Colman didn't know his last name.

Pat Hobby Does His Bit

In order to borrow money gracefully one must choose the time and place. It is a difficult business, for example, when the borrower is cockeyed, or has measles, or a conspicuous shiner. One could continue indefinitely but the inauspicious occasions can be catalogued as one – it is exceedingly difficult to borrow money when one needs it.

Pat Hobby found it difficult in the case of an actor on a set during the shooting of a moving picture. It was about the stiffest chore he had ever undertaken but he was doing it to save his car. To a sordidly commercial glance the jalopy would not have seemed worth saving but, because of Hollywood's great distances, it was an indispensable tool of the writer's trade.

'The finance company – ' explained Pat, but Gyp McCarthy interrupted.

'I got some business in this next take. You want me to blow up on it?'

'I only need twenty,' persisted Pat. 'I can't get jobs if I have to hang around my bedroom.'

'You'd save money that way – you don't get jobs anymore.'

This was cruelly correct. But working or not Pat liked to pass his days in or near a studio. He had reached a dolorous and precarious forty-nine with nothing else to do.

'I got a rewrite job promised for next week,' he lied.

'Oh, nuts to you,' said Gyp. 'You better get off the set before Hilliard sees you.'

Pat glanced nervously toward the group by the camera – then he played his trump card.

'Once – ' he said, ' – once I paid for you to have a baby.'

'Sure you did!' said Gyp wrathfully. 'That was sixteen years ago. And where is it now – it's in jail for running over an old lady without a license.'

'Well I paid for it,' said Pat. 'Two hundred smackers.'

'That's nothing to what it cost me. Would I be stunting at my age if I had dough to lend? Would I be working at all?'

From somewhere in the darkness an assistant director issued an order:

'Ready to go!'

Pat spoke quickly.

'All right,' he said. 'Five bucks.'

'No.'

'All right then,' Pat's red-rimmed eyes tightened. 'I'm going to stand over there and put the hex on you while you say your line.'

'Oh, for God's sake!' said Gyp uneasily. 'Listen, I'll give you five. It's in my coat over there. Here, I'll get it.'

He dashed from the set and Pat heaved a sigh of relief. Maybe Louie, the studio bookie, would let him have ten more.

Again the assistant director's voice:

'Quiet!... We'll take it now!... Lights!'

The glare stabbed into Pat's eyes, blinding him. He took a step the wrong way – then back. Six other people were in the take – a gangster's hide-out – and it seemed that each was in his way.

'All right... Roll 'em... We're turning!'

In his panic Pat had stepped behind a flat which would effectually conceal him. While the actors played their scene he stood there trembling a little, his back hunched

– quite unaware that it was a 'trolley shot', that the camera, moving forward on its track, was almost upon him.

'You by the window – hey you, *Gyp*! hands up.'

Like a man in a dream Pat raised his hands – only then did he realize that he was looking directly into a great black lens – in an instant it also included the English leading woman, who ran past him and jumped out the window. After an interminable second Pat heard the order 'Cut '

Then he rushed blindly through a property door, around a corner, tripping over a cable, recovering himself and tearing for the entrance. He heard footsteps running behind him and increased his gait, but in the doorway itself he was overtaken and turned defensively.

It was the English actress.

'Hurry up!' she cried. 'That finishes my work. I'm flying home to England.'

As she scrambled into her waiting limousine she threw back a last irrelevant remark. 'I'm catching a New York plane in an hour.'

Who cares! Pat thought bitterly, as he scurried away.

He was unaware that her repatriation was to change the course of his life.

II

And he did not have the five – he feared that this particular five was forever out of range. Other means must be found to keep the wolf from the two doors of his coupe. Pat left the lot with despair in his heart, stopping only momentarily to get gas for the car and gin for himself, possibly the last of many drinks they had had together.

Next morning he awoke with an aggravated problem. For once he did not want to go to the studio. It was not merely Gyp McCarthy he feared – it was the whole corporate might of a moving picture company, nay of an industry. Actually to have interfered with the shooting of a movie was somehow a major delinquency, compared to which expensive fumblings on the part of producers or writers went comparatively unpunished.

On the other hand zero hour for the car was the day after tomorrow and Louie, the studio bookie, seemed positively the last resource and a poor one at that.

Nerving himself with an unpalatable snack from the bottom of the bottle, he went to the studio at ten with his coat collar turned up and his hat pulled low over his ears. He knew a sort of underground railway through the make-up department and the commissary kitchen which might get him to Louie's suite unobserved.

Two studio policemen seized him as he rounded the corner by the barber shop.

'Hey, I got a pass!' he protested. 'Good for a week – signed by Jack Berners.'

'Mr Berners specially wants to see you.'

Here it was then – he would be barred from the lot.

'We could sue you!' cried Jack Berners. 'But we couldn't recover.'

'What's one take?' demanded Pat. 'You can use another.'

'No we can't – the camera jammed. And this morning Lily Keatts took a plane to England. She thought she was through.'

'Cut the scene,' suggested Pat – and then on inspiration, 'I bet I could fix it for you.'

'You fixed it, all right!' Berners assured him. 'If there was any way to fix it back I wouldn't have sent for you.'

He paused, looked speculatively at Pat. His buzzer sounded and a secretary's voice said 'Mr Hilliard'.

'Send him in.'

George Hilliard was a huge man and the glance he bent upon Pat was not kindly. But there was some other element besides anger in it and Pat squirmed doubtfully as the two men regarded him with almost impersonal curiosity – as if he were a candidate for a cannibal's frying pan.

'Well, goodbye,' he suggested uneasily.

'What do you think, George?' demanded Berners.

'Well – ' said Hilliard, hesitantly, 'we could black out a couple of teeth.'

Pat rose hurriedly and took a step toward the door, but Hilliard seized him and faced him around.

'Let's hear you talk,' he said.

'You can't beat me up,' Pat clamored. 'You knock my teeth out and I'll sue you.'

There was a pause.

'What do you think?' demanded Berners.

'He can't talk,' said Hilliard.

'You damn right I can talk!' said Pat.

'We can dub three or four lines,' continued Hilliard, 'and nobody'll know the difference. Half the guys you get to play rats can't talk. The point is this one's got the physique and the camera will pull it out of his face too.'

Berners nodded.

'All right, Pat – you're an actor. You've got to play the part this McCarthy had. Only a couple of scenes but they're important. You'll have papers to sign with the Guild and Central Casting and you can report for work this afternoon.'

'What is this!' Pat demanded. 'I'm no ham – ' Remembering that Hilliard had once been a leading man he recoiled from this attitude:'I'm a writer.'

'The character you play is called "The Rat",' continued Berners. He explained why it was necessary for Pat to continue his impromptu appearance of yesterday. The scenes which included Miss Keatts had been shot first, so that she could fulfill an English engagement. But in the filling out of the skeleton it was necessary to show how the gangsters reached their hide-out, and what they did after Miss Keatts dove from the window. Having irrevocably appeared in the shot with Miss Keatts, Pat must appear in half a dozen other shots, to be taken in the next few days.

'What kind of jack is it ?' Pat inquired.

'We were paying McCarthy fifty a day – wait a minute Pat – but I thought I'd pay you your last writing price, two-fifty for the week.'

'How about my reputation ?' objected Pat.

'I won't answer that one,' said Berners. 'But if Benchley can act and Don Stewart and Lewis and Wilder and Woollcott, I guess it won't ruin you.'

Pat drew a long breath.

'Can you let me have fifty on account,' he asked, 'because really I earned that yester – '

'If you got what you earned yesterday you'd be in a hospital. And you're not going on any bat. Here's ten dollars and that's all you see for a week.'

'How about my car – '

'To hell with your car.'

III

'The Rat' was the die-hard of the gang who were engaged in sabotage for an unidentified government of N-zis. His speeches were simplicity itself – Pat had written their like many times. 'Don't finish him till the Brain comes'; Let's get out of here'; 'Fella, you're going out feet first.' Pat found it pleasant – mostly waiting around as in all picture work – and he hoped it might lead to other openings in this line. He was sorry that the job was so short

His last scene was on location. He knew 'The Rat' was to touch off an explosion in which he himself was killed but Pat had watched such scenes and was certain he would be in no slightest danger. Out on the back lot he was mildly curious when they measured him around the waist and chest.

'Making a dummy?' he asked.

'Not exactly,' the prop man said. 'This thing is all made but it was for Gyp McCarthy and I want to see if it'll fit you.'

'Does it?'

'Just exactly.'

'What is it?'

'Well – it's a sort of protector.'

A slight draught of uneasiness blew in Pat's mind.

'Protector for what? Against the explosion?'

'Heck no! The explosion is phony – just a process shot. This is something else.'

'What is it?' persisted Pat. 'If I got to be protected against something I got a right to know what it is.'

Near the false front of a warehouse a battery of cameras were getting into position. George Hilliard came suddenly out of a group and toward Pat and putting his arm on his shoulder steered him toward the actors' dressing tent. Once inside he handed Pat a flask.

'Have a drink, old man.'

Pat took a long pull.

'There's a bit of business, Pat,' Hilliard said, 'needs some new costuming. I'll explain it while they dress you.'

Pat was divested of coat and vest, his trousers were loosened and in an instant a hinged iron doublet was fastened about his middle, extending from his armpits to his crotch very much like a plaster cast.

'This is the very finest strongest iron, Pat,' Hilliard

assured him. 'The very best in tensile strength and resistance. It was built in Pittsburgh.'

Pat suddenly resisted the attempts of two dressers to pull his trousers up over the thing and to slip on his coat and vest.

'What's it for?' he demanded, arms flailing. 'I want to know. You're not going to shoot at me if that's what –'

'No shooting.'

'Then what *is* it? I'm no stunt man –'

'You signed a contract just like McCarthy's to do anything within reason – and our lawyers have certified this.'

'What *is* it?' Pat's mouth was dry.

'It's an automobile.'

'You're going to hit me with an automobile.'

'Give me a chance to tell you,' begged Hilliard. 'Nobody's going to hit you. The auto's going to pass over you, that's all. This case is so strong –'

'Oh no!' said Pat. 'Oh no!' He tore at the iron corselet. 'Not on your –'

George Hilliard pinioned his arms firmly.

'Pat, you almost wrecked this picture once – you're not going to do it again. Be a man.'

'That's what I'm going to be. You're not going to squash me out flat like that extra last month.'

He broke off. Behind Hilliard he saw a face he knew – a hateful and dreaded face – that of the collector for the North Hollywood Finance and Loan Company. Over in the parking lot stood his coupe, faithful pal and servant since 1934, companion of his misfortunes, his only certain home.

'Either you fill your contract,' said George Hilliard, ' – or you're out of pictures for keeps.'

The man from the finance company had taken a step forward. Pat turned to Hilliard.

'Will you loan me – ' he faltered, ' – will you advance me twenty-five dollars?'

'Sure,' said Hilliard.

Pat spoke fiercely to the credit man:

'You hear that? You'll get your money, but if this thing breaks, my death'll be on your head.'

The next few minutes passed in a dream. He heard Hilliard's last instructions as they walked from the tent. Pat was to be lying in a shallow ditch to touch off the dynamite – and then the hero would drive the car slowly across his middle. Pat listened dimly. A picture of himself, cracked like an egg by the factory wall, lay a-thwart his mind.

He picked up the torch and lay down in the ditch. Afar off he heard the call 'Quiet', then Hilliard's voice and the noise of the car warming up.

'Action!' called someone. There was the sound of the car growing nearer – louder. And then Pat Hobby knew no more.

IV

When he awoke it was dark and quiet. For some moments he failed to recognize his whereabouts. Then he saw that stars were out in the California sky and that he was somewhere alone – no – he was held tight in someone's arms. But the arms were of iron and he realized that he was still in the metallic casing. And then it all came back to him – up to the moment when he heard the approach of the car.

As far as he could determine he was unhurt – but why out here and alone?

He struggled to get up but found it was impossible and after a horrified moment he let out a cry for help. For five minutes he called out at intervals until finally a voice came from far away; and assistance arrived in the form of a studio policeman.

'What is it fella ? A drop too much ?'

'Hell no,' cried Pat. 'I was in the shooting this afternoon. It was a lousy trick to go off and leave me in this ditch.'

'They must have forgot you in the excitement.'

'Forgot me! *I* was the excitement. If you don't believe me then feel what I got on!'

The cop helped him to his feet.

'They was upset,' he explained. 'A star don't break his leg every day.'

'What's that ? Did something happen ?'

'Well, as I heard, he was supposed to drive the car at a bump and the car turned over and broke his leg. They had to stop shooting and they're all kind of gloomy.'

'And they leave me inside this – this stove. How do I get it off tonight ? How'm I going to drive my car ?'

But for all his rage Pat felt a certain fierce pride. He was Something in this set-up – someone to be reckoned with after years of neglect. He had managed to hold up the picture once more.

Pat Hobby's Preview

'I haven't got a job for you,' said Berners. 'We've got more writers now than we can use.'

'I didn't ask for a job,' said Pat with dignity. 'But I rate some tickets for the preview tonight – since I got a half credit.'

'Oh yes, I want to talk to you about that,' Berners frowned. 'We may have to take your name off the screen credits.'

'*What?*' exclaimed Pat. 'Why, it's already on! I saw it in the *Reporter*. "By Ward Wainwright and Pat Hobby." '

'But we may have to take it off when we release the picture. Wainwright's back from the East and raising hell. He says that you claimed lines where all you did was change "No" to "No sir" and "crimson" to "red", and stuff like that.'

'I been in this business twenty years,' said Pat. 'I know my rights. That guy laid an egg. I was called in to revise a turkey!'

'You were not,' Berners assured him. 'After Wainwright went to New York I called you in to fix one small character. If I hadn't gone fishing you wouldn't have got away with sticking your name on the script.' Jack Berners broke off, touched by Pat's dismal, red-streaked eyes. 'Still, I was glad to see you get a credit after so long.'

'I'll join the Screen Writers Guild and fight it.'

'You don't stand a chance. Anyhow, Pat, your name's on it tonight at least, and it'll remind everybody you're alive.

And I'll dig you up some tickets – but keep an eye out for
Wainwright. It isn't good for you to get socked if you're
over fifty.'

'I'm in my forties,' said Pat, who was forty-nine.

The Dictograph buzzed. Berners switched it on.

'It's Mr Wainwright.'

'Tell him to wait.' He turned to Pat: 'That's Wainwright.
Better go out the side door.'

'How about the tickets ?'

'Drop by this afternoon.'

To a rising young screen poet this might have been a
crushing blow but Pat was made of sterner stuff. Sterner
not upon himself, but on the harsh fate that had dogged
him for nearly a decade. With all his experience, and with
the help of every poisonous herb that blossoms between
Washington Boulevard and Ventura, between Santa Mon-
ica and Vine – he continued to slip. Sometimes he grabbed
momentarily at a bush, found a few weeks' surcease
upon the island of a 'patch job', but in general the slide
continued at a pace that would have dizzied a lesser
man.

Once safely out of Berners' office, for instance, Pat
looked ahead and not behind. He visioned a drink with
Louie, the studio bookie, and then a call on some old
friends on the lot. Occasionally, but less often every year,
some of these calls developed into jobs before you could
say 'Santa Anita'. But after he had had his drink his eyes
fell upon a lost girl.

She was obviously lost. She stood staring very prettily
at the trucks full of extras that rolled toward the commissary. And then gazed about helpless – so helpless that a
truck was almost upon her when Pat reached out and
plucked her aside.

'Oh, thanks,' she said, 'thanks. I came with a party for

a tour of the studio and a policeman made me leave my camera in some office. Then I went to stage five where the guide said, but it was closed.'

She was a 'Cute Little Blonde'. To Pat's liverish eye, cute little blondes seemed as much alike as a string of paper dolls. Of course they had different names.

'We'll see about it,' said Pat.

'You're very nice. I'm Eleanor Carter from Boise, Idaho.'

He told her his name and that he was a writer. She seemed first disappointed – then delighted.

'A writer ? . . . Oh, of course. I knew they had to have writers but I guess I never heard about one before.'

'Writers get as much as three grand a week,' he assured her firmly. 'Writers are some of the biggest shots in Hollywood.'

'You see, I never thought of it that way.'

'Bernud Shaw was out here,' he said, ' – and Einstein, but they couldn't make the grade.'

They walked to the Bulletin Board and Pat found that there was work scheduled on three stages – and one of the directors was a friend out of the past.

'What did you write ?' Eleanor asked.

A great male Star loomed on the horizon and Eleanor was all eyes till he had passed. Anyhow the names of Pat's pictures would have been unfamiliar to her.

'Those were all silents,' he said.

'Oh. Well, what did you write last ?'

'Well, I worked on a thing at Universal – I don't know what they called it finally – ' He saw that he was not impressing her at all. He thought quickly. What did they know in Boise, Idaho ? 'I wrote *Captains Courageous*,' he said boldly. 'And *Test Pilot* and *Wuthering Heights* and – and *The Awful Truth* and *Mr Smith Goes to Washington*.'

'Oh!' she exclaimed. 'Those are all my favorite pictures.

And *Test Pilot* is my boy friend's favorite picture and *Dark Victory* is mine.'

'I thought *Dark Victory* stank,' he said modestly. 'High-brow stuff,' and he added to balance the scales of truth, 'I been here twenty years.'

They came to a stage and went in. Pat sent his name to the director and they were passed. They watched while Ronald Colman rehearsed a scene.

'Did you write this?' Eleanor whispered.

'They asked me to,' Pat said, 'but I was busy.'

He felt young again, authoritative and active, with a hand in many schemes. Then he remembered something.

'I've got a picture opening tonight.'

'You *have*?'

He nodded.

'I was going to take Claudette Colbert but she's got a cold. Would you like to go?'

II

He was alarmed when she mentioned a family, relieved when she said it was only a resident aunt. It would be like old times walking with a cute little blonde past the staring crowds on the sidewalk. His car was Class of 1933 but he could say it was borrowed – one of his Jap servants had smashed his limousine. Then what? he didn't quite know, but he could put on a good act for one night.

He bought her lunch in the commissary and was so stirred that he thought of borrowing somebody's apartment for the day. There was the old line about 'getting her a test'. But Eleanor was thinking only of getting to a hair-dresser to prepare for tonight, and he escorted her reluctantly to the gate. He had another drink with Louie and went to Jack Berners' office for the tickets.

Berners' secretary had them ready in an envelope.

'We had trouble about these, Mr Hobby.'

'Trouble? Why? Can't a man go to his own preview? Is this something new?'

'It's not that, Mr Hobby,' she said. 'The picture's been talked about so much, every seat is gone.'

Unreconciled, he complained, 'and they just didn't think of me.'

'I'm sorry.' She hesitated. 'These are really Mr Wainwright's tickets. He was so angry about something that he said he wouldn't go – and threw them on my desk. I shouldn't be telling you this.'

'These are *his* seats?'

'Yes, Mr Hobby.'

Pat sucked his tongue. This was in the nature of a triumph. Wainwright had lost his temper, which was the last thing you should ever do in pictures – you could only pretend to lose it – so perhaps his apple-cart wasn't so steady. Perhaps Pat ought to join the Screen Writers Guild and present his case – if the Screen Writers Guild would take him in.

This problem was academic. He was calling for Eleanor at five o'clock and taking her 'somewhere for a cocktail'. He bought a two-dollar shirt, changing into it in the shop and a four-dollar Alpine hat – thus halving his bank account which, since the Bank Holiday of 1933, he carried cautiously in his pocket.

The modest bungalow in West Hollywood yielded up Eleanor without a struggle. On his advice she was not in evening dress but she was as trim and shining as any cute little blonde out of his past. Eager too – running over with enthusiasm and gratitude. He must think of someone whose apartment he could borrow for tomorrow.

'You'd like a test?' he asked as they entered the Brown Derby bar.

'What girl wouldn't?'

'Some wouldn't – for a million dollars.' Pat had had set-backs in his love life. 'Some of them would rather go on pounding the keys or just hanging around. You'd be surprised.'

'I'd do almost anything for a test,' Eleanor said.

Looking at her two hours later he wondered honestly to himself if it couldn't be arranged. There was Harry Gooddorf – there was Jack Berners – but his credit was low on all sides. He could do *something* for her, he decided. He would try at least to get an agent interested – if all went well tomorrow.

'What are you doing tomorrow?' he asked.

'Nothing,' she answered promptly. 'Hadn't we better eat and get to the preview?'

'Sure, sure.'

He made a further inroad on his bank account to pay for his six whiskeys – you certainly had the right to celebrate before your own preview – and took her into the restaurant for dinner. They ate little. Eleanor was too excited – Pat had taken his calories in another form.

It was a long time since he had seen a picture with his name on it. Pat Hobby. As a man of the people he always appeared in the credit titles as Pat Hobby. It would be nice to see it again and though he did not expect his old friends to stand up and sing *Happy Birthday to You*, he was sure there would be back-slapping and even a little turn of attention toward him as the crowd swayed out of the theatre. That would be nice.

'I'm frightened,' said Eleanor as they walked through the alley of packed fans.

'They're looking at you,' he said confidently. 'They look at that pretty pan and try to think if you're an actress.'

A fan shoved an autograph album and pencil toward

Eleanor but Pat moved her firmly along. It was late – the equivalent of 'all aboard' was being shouted around the entrance.

'Show your tickets, please sir.'

Pat opened the envelope and handed them to the doorman. Then he said to Eleanor:

'The seats are reserved – it doesn't matter that we're late.'

She pressed close to him, clinging – it was, as it turned out, the high point of her debut. Less than three steps inside the theatre a hand fell on Pat's shoulder.

'Hey Buddy, these aren't tickets for here.'

Before they knew it they were back outside the door, glared at with suspicious eyes.

'I'm Pat Hobby. I wrote this picture.'

For an instant credulity wandered to his side. Then the hard-boiled doorman sniffed at Pat and stepped in close.

'Buddy you're drunk. These are tickets to another show.'

Eleanor looked and felt uneasy but Pat was cool.

'Go inside and ask Jack Berners,' Pat said. 'He'll tell you.'

'Now listen,' said the husky guard, 'these are tickets for a burlesque down in L.A.' He was steadily edging Pat to the side .'You go to your show, you and your girl friend. And be happy.'

'You don't understand. I wrote this picture.'

'Sure. In a pipe dream.'

'Look at the program. My name's on it. I'm Pat Hobby.'

'Can you prove it ? Let's see your auto license.'

As Pat handed it over he whispered to Eleanor, 'Don't worry!'

'This doesn't say Pat Hobby,' announced the doorman. 'This says the car's owned by the North Hollywood Finance and Loan Company. Is that you ?'

For once in his life Pat could think of nothing to say –

he cast one quick glance at Eleanor. Nothing in her face indicated that he was anything but what he thought he was – all alone.

III

Though the preview crowd had begun to drift away, with that vague American wonder as to why they had come at all, one little cluster found something arresting and poignant in the faces of Pat and Eleanor. They were obviously gate-crashers, outsiders like themselves, but the crowd resented the temerity of their effort to get in – a temerity which the crowd did not share. Little jeering jests were audible. Then, with Eleanor already edging away from the distasteful scene, there was a flurry by the door. A well-dressed six-footer strode out of the theatre and stood gazing till he saw Pat.

'There you are!' he shouted.

Pat recognized Ward Wainwright.

'Go in and look at it!' Wainwright roared. 'Look at it. Here's some ticket stubs ! I think the prop boy directed it! Go and look!' To the doorman he said: 'It's all right! *He* wrote it. I wouldn't have my name on an inch of it.'

Trembling with frustration, Wainwright threw up his hands and strode off into the curious crowd.

Eleanor was terrified. But the same spirit that had inspired 'I'd do anything to get in the movies', kept her standing there – though she felt invisible fingers reaching forth to drag her back to Boise. She had been intending to run – hard and fast. The hard-boiled doorman and the tall stranger had crystallized her feelings that Pat was 'rather simple'. She would never let those red-rimmed eyes come close to her – at least for any more than a doorstep kiss. She was saving herself for somebody – and it wasn't Pat. Yet she felt that the lingering crowd was a tribute to her

– such as she had never exacted before. Several times she threw a glance at the crowd – a glance that now changed from wavering fear into a sort of queenliness.

She felt exactly like a star.

Pat, too, was all confidence. This was *his* preview; all had been delivered into his hands: his name would stand alone on the screen when the picture was released. There had to be *some*body's name, didn't there? – and Wainwright had withdrawn.

SCREENPLAY BY PAT HOBBY.

He seized Eleanor's elbow in a firm grasp and steered her triumphantly towards the door:

'Cheer up, baby. That's the way it is. You see?'

No Harm Trying

Pat Hobby's apartment lay athwart a delicatessen shop on Wilshire Boulevard. And there lay Pat himself, surrounded by his books – the *Motion Picture Almanac* of 1928 and *Barton's Track Guide, 1939* – by his pictures, authentically signed photographs of Mabel Normand and Barbara La-Marr (who, being deceased, had no value in the pawn shops) – and by his dogs in their cracked leather oxfords, perched on the arm of a slanting settee.

Pat was at 'the end of his resources' – though this term is too ominous to describe a fairly usual condition in his life. He was an old timer in pictures; he had once known sumptuous living, but for the past ten years jobs had been hard to hold – harder to hold than glasses.

'Think of it,' he often mourned. 'Only a writer – at forty-nine.'

All this afternoon he had turned the pages of *The Times* and *The Examiner* for an idea. Though he did not intend to compose a motion picture from this idea, he needed it to get him inside a studio. If you had nothing to submit it was increasingly difficult to pass the gate. But though these two newspapers, together with *Life*, were the sources most commonly combed for 'originals', they yielded him nothing this afternoon. There were wars, a fire in Topanga Canyon, press releases from the studios, municipal corruptions, and always the redeeming deeds of 'The Trojuns', but Pat found nothing that competed in human interest with the betting page.

– If I could get out to Santa Anita, he thought – I could maybe get an idea about the nags.

This cheering idea was interrupted by his landlord, from the delicatessen store below.

'I told you I wouldn't deliver any more messages,' said Nick, 'and *still* I won't. But Mr Carl Le Vigne is telephoning in person from the studio and wants you should go over right away.'

The prospect of a job did something to Pat. It anesthetized the crumbled, struggling remnants of his manhood, and inoculated him instead with a bland, easy-going confidence. The set speeches and attitudes of success returned to him. His manner as he winked at a studio policeman, stopped to chat with Louie, the bookie, and presented himself to Mr Le Vigne's secretary, indicated that he had been engaged with momentous tasks in other parts of the globe. By saluting Le Vigne with a facetious 'Hel-*lo* Captain!' he behaved almost as an equal, a trusted lieutenant who had never really been away.

'Pat, your wife's in the hospital,' Le Vigne said. 'It'll probably be in the papers this afternoon.'

Pat started.

'My wife?' he said. 'What wife?'

'Estelle. She tried to cut her wrists.'

'Estelle!' Pat exclaimed, 'You mean E*stelle*? Say, I was only married to her three weeks!'

'She was the best girl you ever had,' said Le Vigne grimly.

'I haven't even heard of her for ten years.'

'You're hearing about her now. They called all the studios trying to locate you.'

'I had nothing to do with it.'

'I know – she's only been here a week. She had a run of hard luck wherever it was she lived – New Orleans? Husband died, child died, no money . . .'

Pat breathed easier. They weren't trying to hang anything on him.

'Anyhow she'll live,' Le Vigne reassured him superflu-
ously, ' – and she was the best script girl on the lot once.
We'd like to take care of her. We thought the way was
give you a job. Not exactly a job, because I know you're
not up to it.' He glanced into Pat's red-rimmed eyes. 'More
of a sinecure.'

Pat became uneasy. He didn't recognize the word, but
'sin' disturbed him and 'cure' brought a whole flood of
unpleasant memories.

'You're on the payroll at two-fifty a week for three
weeks,' said Le Vigne, ' – but one-fifty of that goes to the
hospital for your wife's bill.'

'But we're divorced!' Pat protested. 'No Mexican stuff
either. I've been married since, and so has – '

'Take it or leave it. You can have an office here, and if
anything you can do comes up we'll let you know.'

'I never worked for a hundred a week.'

'We're not asking you to work. If you want you can stay
home.'

Pat reversed his field.

'Oh, I'll work,' he said quickly. 'You dig me up a good
story and I'll show you whether I can work or not.'

Le Vigne wrote something on a slip of paper.

'All right. They'll find you an office.'

Outside Pat looked at the memorandum.

'Mrs John Devlin,' it read, 'Good Samaritan Hospital.'

The very words irritated him.

'Good Samaritan!' he exclaimed, 'Good gyp joint! One
hundred and fifty bucks a week.'

II

Pat had been given many a charity job but this was the

first one that made him feel ashamed. He did not mind not *earn*ing his salary, but not getting it was another matter. And he wondered if other people on the lot who were obviously doing nothing, were being fairly paid for it. There were, for example, a number of beautiful young ladies who walked aloof as stars, and whom Pat took for stock girls, until Eric, the callboy, told him they were imports from Vienna and Budapest, not yet cast for pictures. Did half their pay-checks go to keep husbands they had only had for three weeks?

The loveliest of these was Lizzette Starheim, a violet-eyed little blonde with an ill-concealed air of disillusion. Pat saw her alone at tea almost every afternoon in the commissary – and made her acquaintance one day by simply sliding into a chair opposite.

'Hello, Lizzette,' he said. 'I'm Pat Hobby, the writer.'

'Oh, hello!'

She flashed such a dazzling smile that for a moment he thought she must have heard of him.

'When they going to cast you?' he demanded.

'I don't know.' Her accent was faint and poignant.

'Don't let them give you the run-around. Not with a face like yours.' Her beauty roused a rusty eloquence. 'Sometimes they just keep you under contract till your teeth fall out, because you look too much like their big star.'

'Oh no,' she said distressfully.

'Oh yes!' he assured her, 'I'm telling *you*. Why don't you go to another company and get borrowed? Have you thought of that idea?'

'I think it's wonderful.'

He intended to go further into the subject but Miss Starheim looked at her watch and got up.

'I must go now, Mr –'

'Hobby. Pat Hobby.'

Pat joined Dutch Waggoner, the director, who was shooting dice with a waitress at another table.

'Between pictures, Dutch ?'

'Between pictures hell!' said Dutch. 'I haven't done a picture for six months and my contract's got six months to run. I'm trying to break it. Who was the little blonde ?'

Afterwards, back in his office, Pat discussed these encounters with Eric the callboy.

'All signed up and no place to go,' said Eric. 'Look at this Jeff Manfred, now – an associate producer! Sits in his office and sends notes to the big shots – and I carry back word they're in Palm Springs. It breaks my heart. Yesterday he put his head on his desk and boo-hoo'd.'

'What's the answer ?' asked Pat.

'Changa management,' suggested Eric, darkly. 'Shake-up coming.'

'Who's going to the top ?' Pat asked, with scarcely concealed excitement.

'Nobody knows,' said Eric. 'But wouldn't I like to land up-hill! Boy! I want a writer's job. I got three ideas so new they're wet behind the ears.'

'It's no life at all,' Pat assured him with conviction. 'I'd trade with you right now.'

In the hall next day he intercepted Jeff Manfred who walked with the unconvincing hurry of one without a destination.

'What's the rush, Jeff ?' Pat demanded, falling into step.

'Reading some scripts,' Jeff panted without conviction.

Pat drew him unwillingly into his office.

'Jeff, have you heard about the shake-up ?'

'Listen now, Pat – ' Jeff looked nervously at the walls. 'What shake-up ?' he demanded.

'I heard that this Harmon Shaver is going to be the new boss,' ventured Pat, 'Wall Street control.'

'Harmon Shaver!' Jeff scoffed. 'He doesn't know anything about pictures – he's just a money man. He wanders around like a lost soul.' Jeff sat back and considered. 'Still – if you're *right*, he'd be a man you could get to.' He turned mournful eyes on Pat. 'I haven't been able to see Le Vigne or Barnes or Bill Behrer for a month. Can't get an assignment, can't get an actor, can't get a story.' He broke off. 'I've thought of drumming up something on my own. Got any ideas?'

'Have I?' said Pat. 'I got three ideas so new they're wet behind the ears.'

'Who for?'

'Lizzette Starheim,' said Pat, 'with Dutch Waggoner directing – see?'

III

'I'm with you all a hundred per cent,' said Harmon Shaver. 'This is the most encouraging experience I've had in pictures.' He had a bright bond-salesman's chuckle. 'By God, it reminds me of a circus we got up when I was a boy.'

They had come to his office inconspicuously like conspirators – Jeff Manfred, Waggoner, Miss Starheim and Pat Hobby.

'You like the idea, Miss Starheim?' Shaver continued.

'I think it's wonderful.'

'And you, Mr Waggoner?'

'I've heard only the general line,' said Waggoner with director's caution, 'but it seems to have the old emotional socko.' He winked at Pat. 'I didn't know this old tramp had it in him.'

Pat glowed with pride. Jeff Manfred, though he was elated, was less sanguine.

'It's important nobody talks,' he said nervously. 'The Big Boys would find some way of killing it. In a week, when we've got the script done we'll go to them.'

'I agree,' said Shaver. 'They have run the studio so long that, well, I don't trust my own secretaries – I sent them to the races this afternoon.'

Back in Pat's office Eric, the callboy, was waiting. He did not know that he was the hinge upon which swung a great affair.

'You like the stuff, eh?' he asked eagerly.

'Pretty good,' said Pat with calculated indifference.

'You said you'd pay more for the next batch.'

'Have a heart!' Pat was aggrieved. 'How many callboys get seventy-five a week?'

'How many callboys can write?'

Pat considered. Out of the two hundred a week Jeff Manfred was advancing from his own pocket, he had naturally awarded himself a commission of sixty per cent.

'I'll make it a hundred,' he said. 'Now check yourself off the lot and meet me in front of Benny's bar.'

At the hospital, Estelle Hobby Devlin sat up in bed, over-whelmed by the unexpected visit.

'I'm glad you came, Pat,' she said, 'you've been very kind. Did you get my note?'

'Forget it,' Pat said gruffly. He had never liked this wife. She had loved him too much – until she found suddenly that he was a poor lover. In her presence he felt inferior.

'I got a guy outside,' he said.

'What for?'

'I thought maybe you had nothing to do and you might want to pay me back for all this jack – '

He waved his hand around the bare hospital room.

'You were a swell script girl once. Do you think if I got

a typewriter you could put some good stuff into continuity?'

'Why – yes. I suppose I could.'

'It's a secret. We can't trust anybody at the studio.'

'All right,' she said.

'I'll send this kid in with the stuff. I got a conference.'

'All right – and – oh Pat – come and see me again.'

'Sure, I'll come.'

But he knew he wouldn't. He didn't like sick rooms –
he lived in one himself. From now on he was done with
poverty and failure. He admired strength – he was taking
Lizzette Starheim to a wrestling match that night.

IV

In his private musings Harmon Shaver referred to the
showdown as 'the surprise party'. He was going to con-
front Le Vigne with a *fait accompli* and he gathered his
coterie before phoning Le Vigne to come over to his office.

'What for?' demanded Le Vigne. 'Couldn't you tell me
now – I'm busy as hell.'

This arrogance irritated Shaver – who was here to watch
over the interest of Eastern stockholders.

'I don't ask much,' he said sharply. 'I let you fellows
laugh at me behind my back and freeze me out of things.
But now I've got something and I'd like you to come over.'

'All right – all right.'

Le Vigne's eyebrows lifted as he saw the members of the
new production unit but he said nothing – sprawled into
an arm chair with his eyes on the floor and his fingers over
his mouth.

Mr Shaver came around the desk and poured forth
words that had been fermenting in him for months. Sim-
mered to its essentials, his protest was: 'You would not
let me play, but I'm going to play anyhow.' Then he

nodded to Jeff Manfred – who opened the script and read aloud. This took an hour, and still Le Vigne sat motionless and silent.

'There you are,' said Shaver triumphantly. 'Unless you've got any objection I think we ought to assign a budget to this proposition and get going. I'll answer to my people.'

Le Vigne spoke at last.

'You like it, Miss Starheim?'

'I think it's wonderful.'

'What language you going to play it in?'

To everyone's surprise Miss Starheim got to her feet.

'I must go now,' she said with her faint poignant accent.

'Sit down and answer me,' said Le Vigne. 'What language are you playing it in?'

Miss Starheim looked tearful.

'Wenn I gute teachers hätte konnte ich dann thees role gut spielen,' she faltered.

'But you like the script.'

She hesitated.

'I think it's wonderful.'

Le Vigne turned to the others.

'Miss Starheim has been here eight months,' he said. 'She's had three teachers. Unless things have changed in the past two weeks she can say just three sentences. She can say, "How do you do"; she can say "I think it's wonderful"; and she can say "I must go now." Miss Starheim has turned out to be a pinhead – I'm not insulting her because she doesn't know what it means. Anyhow – there's your Star.'

He turned to Dutch Waggoner, but Dutch was already on his feet.

'Now Carl –' he said defensively.

'You force me to it,' said Le Vigne. 'I've trusted drunks up to a point, but I'll be goddam if I'll trust a hophead.'

He turned to Harmon Shaver.

'Dutch has been good for exactly one week apiece on his last four pictures. He's all right now but as soon as the heat goes on he reaches for the little white powders. Now Dutch! Don't say anything you'll regret. We're carrying you in *hopes* – but you won't get on a stage till we've had a doctor's certificate for a year.'

Again he turned to Harmon.

'There's your director. Your supervisor, Jeff Manfred, is here for one reason only – because he's Behrer's wife's cousin. There's nothing against him but he belongs to silent days as much as – as much as – ' His eyes fell upon a quavering broken man, ' – as much as Pat Hobby.'

'What do you mean?' demanded Jeff.

'You trusted Hobby, didn't you? That tells the whole story.' He turned back to Shaver. 'Jeff's a weeper and a wisher and a dreamer. Mr Shaver, you have bought a lot of condemned building material.'

'Well, I've bought a good story,' said Shaver defiantly.

'Yes. That's right. We'll make that story.'

'Isn't that something?' demanded Shaver. 'With all this secrecy how was I to know about Mr Waggoner and Miss Starheim? But I do know a good story.'

'Yes,' said Le Vigne absently. He got up. 'Yes – it's a good story . . . Come along to my office, Pat.'

He was already at the door. Pat cast an agonized look at Mr Shaver as if for support. Then, weakly, he followed.

'Sit down, Pat.'

'That Eric's got talent, hasn't he?' said Le Vigne. 'He'll go places. How'd you come to dig him up?'

Pat felt the straps of the electric chair being adjusted.

'Oh – I just dug him up. He – came in my office.'

'We're putting him on salary,' said Le Vigne. 'We ought to have some system to give these kids a chance.'

He took a call on his Dictograph, then swung back to Pat.

'But how did you ever get mixed up with this goddam Shaver. *You*, Pat – an old timer like you.'

'Well, I thought – '

'Why doesn't he go back East?' continued Le Vigne disgustedly. 'Getting all you poops stirred up!'

Blood flowed back into Pat's veins. He recognized his signal, his dog-call.

'Well, I got you a story, didn't I?' he said, with almost a swagger. And he added, 'How'd you know about it?'

'I went down to see Estelle in the hospital. She and this kid were working on it. I walked right in on them.'

'Oh,' said Pat.

'I knew the kid by sight. Now, Pat, tell me this – did Jeff Manfred think you wrote it – or was he in on the racket?'

'Oh God,' Pat mourned. 'What do I have to answer that for?'

Le Vigne leaned forward intensely.

'Pat, you're sitting over a trap door!' he said with savage eyes. 'Do you see how the carpet's cut? I just have to press this button and drop you down to hell! Will you *talk*?'

Pat was on his feet, staring wildly at the floor.

'Sure I will!' he cried. He believed it – he believed such things.

'All right,' said Le Vigne relaxing. 'There's whiskey in the sideboard there. Talk quick and I'll give you another month at two-fifty. I kinda like having you around.'

A Patriotic Short

Pat Hobby, the writer and the man, had his great success in Hollywood during what Irvin Cobb refers to as 'the mosaic swimming-pool age – just before the era when they had to have a shinbone of St Sebastian for a clutch lever.'

Mr Cobb no doubt exaggerates, for when Pat had his pool in those fat days of silent pictures, it was entirely cement, unless you should count the cracks where the water stubbornly sought its own level through the mud.

'But it *was* a pool,' he assured himself one afternoon more than a decade later. Though he was now more than grateful for this small chore he had assigned him by producer Berners – one week at two-fifty – all the insolence of office could not take that memory away.

He had been called in to the studio to work upon an humble short. It was based on the career of General Fitzhugh Lee who fought for the Confederacy and later for the U.S.A. against Spain – so it would offend neither North nor South. And in the recent conference Pat had tried to co-operate.

'I was thinking – ' he suggested to Jack Berners ' – that it might be a good thing if we could give it a Jewish touch.'

'What do you mean?' demanded Jack Berners quickly.

'Well I thought – the way things are and all, it would be a sort of good thing to show that there were a number of Jews in it too.'

'In what?'

'In the Civil War.' Quickly he reviewed his meager history. 'They were, weren't they?'

'Naturally,' said Berners, with some impatience, 'I suppose everybody was except the Quakers.'

'Well, my idea was that we could have this Fitzhugh Lee in love with a Jewish girl. He's going to be shot at curfew so she grabs a church bell – '

Jack Berners leaned forward earnestly.

'Say, Pat, you want this job, don't you? Well, I told you the story. You got the first script. If you thought up this tripe to please me you're losing your grip.'

Was that a way to treat a man who had once owned a pool which had been talked about by –

That was how he happened to be thinking about his long lost swimming pool as he entered the shorts department. He was remembering a certain day over a decade ago in all its details, how he had arrived at the studio in his car driven by a Filipino in uniform; the deferential bow of the guard at the gate which had admitted car and all to the lot, his ascent to that long lost office which had a room for the secretary and was really a director's office . . .

His reverie was broken off by the voice of Ben Brown, head of the shorts department, who walked him into his own chambers.

'Jack Berners just phoned me,' he said. 'We don't want any new angles, Pat. We've got a good story. Fitzhugh Lee was a dashing cavalry commander. He was a nephew of Robert E. Lee and we want to show him at Appomattox, pretty bitter and all that. And then show how he became reconciled – we'll have to be careful because Virginia is swarming with Lees – and how he finally accepts a U.S. commission from President McKinley – '

Pat's mind darted back again into the past. The President

– that was the magic word that had gone around that
morning many years ago. The President of the United
States was going to make a visit to the lot. Everyone had
been agog about it – it seemed to mark a new era in pictures because a President of the United States had never
visited a studio before. The executives of the company
were all dressed up – from a window of his long lost Beverly Hills house Pat had seen Mr Maranda, whose mansion
was next door to him, bustle down his walk in a cutaway
coat at nine o'clock, and had known that something was
up. He thought maybe it was clergy but when he reached
the lot he had found it was the President of the United
States himself who was coming . . .

'Clean up the stuff about Spain,' Ben Brown was saying.
'The guy that wrote it was a Red and he's got all the Spanish officers with ants in their pants. Fix up that.'

In the office assigned him Pat looked at the script of
True to Two Flags. The first scene showed General Fitzhugh Lee at the head of his cavalry receiving word that
Petersburg had been evacuated. In the script Lee took the
blow in pantomime, but Pat was getting two-fifty a week
– so, casually and without effort, he wrote in one of his
favorite lines:

Lee (to his officers)
Well, what are you standing here gawking for? DO *something!*

6. *Medium Shot Officers pepping up, slapping each other on
back, etc.*

Dissolve to:

To what? Pat's mind dissolved once more into the glamorous past. On that happy day in the twenties his phone
had rung at about noon. It had been Mr Maranda.

'Pat, the President is lunching in the private dining room.

Doug Fairbanks can't come so there's a place empty and anyhow we think there ought to be one writer there.'

His memory of the luncheon was palpitant with glamor. The Great Man had asked some questions about pictures and had told a joke and Pat had laughed and laughed with the others – all of them solid men together – rich, happy and successful.

Afterwards the President was to go on some sets and see some scenes taken and still later he was going to Mr Maranda's house to meet some of the women stars at tea. Pat was not invited to that party but he went home early anyhow and from his veranda saw the cortège drive up, with Mr Maranda beside the President in the back seat. Ah he was proud of pictures then – of his position in them – of the President of the happy country where he was born. . .

Returning to reality Pat looked down at the script of *True to Two Flags* and wrote slowly and thoughtfully: *Insert: A calendar – with the years plainly marked and the sheets blowing off in a cold wind, to show Fitzhugh Lee growing older and older.*

His labors had made him thirsty – not for water, but he knew better than to take anything else his first day on the job. He got up and went out into the hall and along the corridor to the water-cooler.

As he walked he slipped back into his reverie.

That had been a lovely California afternoon so Mr Maranda had taken his exalted guest and the coterie of stars into his garden, which adjoined Pat's garden. Pat had gone out his back door and followed a low privet hedge keeping out of sight – and then accidentally come face to face with the Presidential party.

The President had smiled and nodded. Mr Maranda smiled and nodded.

'You met Mr Hobby at lunch,' Mr Maranda said to the President. 'He's one of our writers.'

'Oh yes,' said the President, 'you write the pictures.'

'Yes I do,' said Pat.

The President glanced over into Pat's property.

'I suppose – ' he said, ' – that you get lots of inspiration sitting by the side of that fine pool.'

'Yes,' said Pat, 'yes, I do.'

... Pat filled his cup at the cooler. Down the hall there was a group approaching – Jack Berners, Ben Brown and several other executives and with them a girl to whom they were very attentive and deferential. He recognized her face – she was the girl of the year, the It girl, the Oomph girl, the Glamour Girl, the girl for whose services every studio was in violent competition.

Pat lingered over his drink. He had seen many phonies break in and break out again, but this girl was the real thing, someone to stir every pulse in the nation. He felt his own heart beat faster. Finally, as the procession drew near, he put down the cup, dabbed at his hair with his hand and took a step out into the corridor.

The girl looked at him – he looked at the girl. Then she took one arm of Jack Berners' and one of Ben Brown's and suddenly the party seemed to walk right through him – so that he had to take a step back against the wall.

An instant later Jack Berners turned around and said back to him, 'Hello, Pat.' And then some of the others threw half glances around but no one else spoke, so interested were they in the girl.

In his office, Pat looked at the scene where President McKinley offers a United States commission to Fitzhugh Lee. Suddenly he gritted his teeth and bore down on his pencil as he wrote:

Lee

Mr President, you can take your commission and go straight
to hell.

Then he bent down over his desk, his shoulders shaking
as he thought of that happy day when he had had a swimming pool.

On the Trail of Pat Hobby

The day was dark from the outset, and a California fog crept everywhere. It had followed Pat in his headlong, hatless flight across the city. His destination, his refuge, was the studio, where he was not employed but which had been home to him for twenty years.

Was it his imagination or did the policeman at the gate give him and his pass an especially long look? It might be the lack of a hat – Hollywood was full of hatless men but Pat felt marked, especially as there had been no opportunity to part his thin grey hair.

In the writers' building he went into the lavatory. Then he remembered: by some inspired ukase from above, all mirrors had been removed from the writers' building a year ago.

Across the hall he saw Bee McIlvaine's door ajar, and discerned her plump person.

'Bee, can you loan me your compact box?' he asked.

Bee looked at him suspiciously, then frowned and dug it from her purse.

'You on the lot?' she inquired.

'Will be next week,' he prophesied. He put the compact on her desk and bent over it with his comb. 'Why won't they put mirrors back in the johnnies? Do they think writers would look at themselves all day?'

'Remember when they took out the couches?' said Bee. 'In nineteen thirty-two. And they put them back in thirty-four.'

'I worked at home,' said Pat feelingly.

Finished with her mirror he wondered if she were good for a loan– enough to buy a hat and something to eat. Bee must have seen the look in his eyes for she forestalled him.

'The Finns got all my money,' she said, 'and I'm worried about my job. Either my picture starts tomorrow or it's going to be shelved. We haven't even got a title.'

She handled him a mimeographed bulletin from the scenario department and Pat glanced at the headline.

TO ALL DEPARTMENTS
  TITLE WANTED – FIFTY DOLLARS REWARD
    SUMMARY FOLLOWS

'I could use fifty,' Pat said. 'What's it about?'

'It's written there. It's about a lot of stuff that goes on in tourist cabins.'

Pat started and looked at her wild-eyed. He had thought to be safe here behind the guarded gates but news traveled fast. This was a friendly or perhaps not so friendly warning. He must move on. He was a hunted man now, with nowhere to lay his hatless head.

'I don't know anything about that,' he mumbled and walked hastily from the room.

II

Just inside the door of the commissary Pat looked around. There was no guardian except the girl at the cigarette stand but obtaining another person's hat was subject to one complication: it was hard to judge the size by a cursory glance, while the sight of a man trying on several hats in a check room was unavoidably suspicious.

Personal taste also obtruded itself. Pat was beguiled by a green fedora with a sprightly feather but it was too readily identifiable. This was also true of a fine white

Stetson for the open spaces. Finally he decided on a sturdy grey Homberg which looked as if it would give him good service. With trembling hands he put it on. It fitted. He walked out – in painful, interminable slow motion.

His confidence was partly restored in the next hour by the fact that no one he encountered made references to tourists' cabins. It had been a lean three months for Pat. He had regarded his job as night clerk for the Selecto Tourists Cabins as a mere fill-in, never to be mentioned to his friends. But when the police squad came this morning they held up the raid long enough to assure Pat, or Don Smith as he called himself, that he would be wanted as a witness. The story of his escape lies in the realm of melodrama, how he went out a side door, bought a half pint of what he so desperately needed at the corner drugstore, hitch-hiked his way across the great city, going limp at the sight of traffic cops and only breathing free when he saw the studio's high-flown sign.

After a call on Louie, the studio bookie, whose great patron he once had been, he dropped in on Jack Berners. He had no idea to submit, but he caught Jack in a hurried moment flying off to a producers' conference and was unexpectedly invited to step in and wait for his return.

The office was rich and comfortable. There were no letters worth reading on the desk, but there were a decanter and glasses in a cupboard and presently he lay down on a big soft couch and fell asleep.

He was awakened by Berners' return, in high indignation.

'Of all the damn nonsense! We get a hurry call – heads of all departments. One man is late and we wait for him. He comes in and gets a bawling out for wasting thousands of dollars worth of time. Then what do you suppose: Mr Marcus has lost his favorite hat!'

Pat failed to associate the fact with himself.

'All the department heads stop production!' continued Berners. 'Two thousand people look for a grey Homberg hat!' He sank despairingly into a chair. 'I can't talk to you today, Pat. By four o'clock, I've got to get a title to a picture about a tourist camp. Got an idea?'

'No,' said Pat. 'No.'

'Well, go up to Bee McIlvaine's office and help her figure something out. There's fifty dollars in it.'

In a daze Pat wandered to the door.

'Hey,' said Berners, 'don't forget your hat.'

III

Feeling the effects of his day outside the law, and of a tumbler full of Berners' brandy, Pat sat in Bee McIlvaine's office.

'We've got to get a title,' said Bee gloomily.

She handed Pat the mimeograph offering fifty dollars reward and put a pencil in his hand. Pat stared at the paper unseeingly.

'How about it?' she asked. 'Who's got a title?'

There was a long silence.

'*Test Pilot*'s been used, hasn't it?' he said with a vague tone.

'Wake up! This isn't about aviation.'

'Well, I was just thinking it was a good title.'

'So's *The Birth of a Nation*.'

'But not for this picture,' Pat muttered. '*Birth of a Nation* wouldn't suit this picture.'

'Are you ribbing me?' demanded Bee. 'Or are you losing your mind? This is serious.'

'Sure – I know.' Feebly he scrawled words at the bottom of the page. 'I've had a couple of drinks that's all. My head'll clear up in a minute. I'm trying to think what have been the most successful titles. The trouble is they've all been used, like *It Happened One Night*.'

Bee looked at him uneasily. He was having trouble keeping his eyes open and she did not want him to pass out in her office. After a minute she called Jack Berners.

'Could you possibly come up? I've got some title ideas.'

Jack arrived with a sheaf of suggestions sent in from here and there in the studio, but digging through them yielded no ore.

'How about it, Pat? Got anything?'

Pat braced himself to an effort.

'I like *It Happened One Morning*,' he said – then looked desperately at his scrawl on the mimeograph paper, 'or else – *Grand Motel*.'

Berners smiled.

'*Grand Motel*,' he repeated. 'By God! I think you've got something. *Grand Motel*.'

'I said *Grand Hotel*,' said Pat.

'No, you didn't. You said *Grand Motel* – and for my money it wins the fifty.'

'I've got to go lie down,' announced Pat. 'I feel sick.'

'There's an empty office across the way. That's a funny idea Pat, *Grand Motel* – or else *Motel Clerk*. How do you like that?'

As the fugitive quickened his step out the door Bee pressed the hat into his hands.

'Good work, old timer,' she said.

Pat seized Mr Marcus' hat, and stood holding it there like a bowl of soup.

'Feel – better – now,' he mumbled after a moment. 'Be back for the money.'

And carrying his burden he shambled toward the lavatory.

Fun in an Artist's Studio

This was back in 1938 when few people except the Germans knew that they had already won their war in Europe. People still cared about art and tried to make it out of everything from old clothes to orange peel and that was how the Princess Dignanni found Pat. She wanted to make art out of him.

'No, not you, Mr DeTinc.' she said, 'I can't paint you. You are a very standardized product, Mr DeTinc.'

Mr DeTinc, who was a power in pictures and had even been photographed with Mr Duchman, the Secret Sin specialist, stepped smoothly out of the way. He was not offended – in his whole life Mr DeTinc had never been offended – but especially not now, for the Princess did not want to paint Clark Gable or Spencer Rooney or Vivien Leigh either.

She saw Pat in the commissary and found he was a writer, and asked that he be invited to Mr DeTinc's party. The Princess was a pretty woman born in Boston, Massachusetts and Pat was forty-nine with red-rimmed eyes and a soft purr of whiskey on his breath.

'You write scenarios, Mr Hobby?'

'I help,' said Pat. 'Takes more than one person to prepare a script.'

He was flattered by this attention and not a little suspicious. It was only because his supervisor was a nervous wreck that he happened to have a job at all. His supervisor had forgotten a week ago that he had hired Pat, and when

Pat was spotted in the commissary and told he was wanted at Mr DeTinc's house, the writer had passed a *mauvais quart d'heure*. It did not even look like the kind of party that Pat had known in his prosperous days. There was not so much as a drunk passed out in the downstairs toilet.

'I imagine scenario writing is very well-paid,' said the Princess.

Pat glanced around to see who was within hearing. Mr DeTinc had withdrawn his huge bulk somewhat, but one of his apparently independent eyes seemed fixed glittering on Pat.

'Very well paid,' said Pat – and he added in a lower voice, ' – if you can get it.'

The Princess seemed to understand and lowered her voice too.

'You mean writers have trouble getting work ?'

He nodded.

'Too many of 'em get in these unions.' He raised his voice a little for Mr DeTinc's benefit. 'They're all Reds, most of these writers.'

The Princess nodded.

'Will you turn your face a little to the light ?' she said politely. 'There, that's fine. You won't mind coming to my studio tomorrow, will you ? Just to pose for me an hour ?'

He scrutinized her again.

'Naked ?' he asked cautiously.

'Oh, no,' she averred. 'Just the head.'

Mr DeTinc moved nearer and nodded.

'You ought to go. Princess Dignanni is going to paint some of the biggest stars here. Going to paint Jack Benny and Baby Sandy and Hedy Lamarr – isn't that a fact. Princess ?'

The artist didn't answer. She was a pretty good portrait

painter and she knew just how good she was and just how much of it was her title. She was hesitating between her several manners – Picasso's rose period with a flash of Boldini, or straight Reginald Marsh. But she knew what she was going to call it. She was going to call it Hollywood and Vine.

II

In spite of the reassurance that he would be clothed Pat approached the rendezvous with uneasiness. In his young and impressionable years he had looked through a peephole into a machine where two dozen postcards slapped before his eyes in sequence. The story unfolded was *Fun in an Artist's Studio*. Even now with the strip tease a legalized municipal project, he was a little shocked at the remembrance, and when he presented himself next day at the Princess' bungalow at the Beverly Hills Hotel it would not have surprised him if she had met him in a turkish towel. He was disappointed. She wore a smock and her black hair was brushed straight back like a boy's.

Pat had stopped off for a couple of drinks on the way, but his first words: 'How'ya Duchess?' failed to set a jovial note for the occasion.

'Well, Mr Hobby,' she said cooly, 'it's nice of you to spare me an afternoon.'

'We don't work too hard in Hollywood,' he assured her. 'Everything is "Manana" – in Spanish that means tomorrow.'

She led him forthwith into a rear apartment where an easel stood on a square of canvas by the window. There was a couch and they sat down.

'I want to get used to you for a minute,' she said. 'Did you ever pose before?'

'Do I look that way?' He winked, and when she smiled

he felt better and asked: 'You haven't got a drink around, have you?'

The Princess hesitated. She had wanted him to look as if he *needed* one. Compromising, she went to the ice box and fixed him a small highball. She returned to find that he had taken off his coat and tie and lay informally upon the couch.

'That *is* better,' the Princess said. 'That shirt you're wearing. I think they make them for Hollywood – like the special prints they make for Ceylon and Guatemala. Now drink this and we'll get to work.'

'Why don't you have a drink too and make it friendly?' Pat suggested.

'I had one in the pantry,' she lied.

'Married woman?' he asked.

'I have been married. Now would you mind sitting on this stool?'

Reluctantly Pat got up, took down the highball, somewhat thwarted by the thin taste, and moved to the stool. 'Now sit very still,' she said.

He sat silent as she worked. It was three o'clock. They were running the third race at Santa Anita and he had ten bucks on the nose. That made sixty he owed Louie, the studio bookie, and Louie stood determinedly beside him at the pay window every Thursday. This dame had good legs under the easel – her red lips pleased him and the way her bare arms moved as she worked. Once upon a time he wouldn't have looked at a woman over twenty-five, unless it was a secretary right in the office with him. But the kids you saw around now were snooty – always talking about calling the police.

'Please sit still, Mr Hobby.'

'What say we knock off,' he suggested. 'This work makes you thirsty.'

The Princess had been painting half an hour. Now she stopped and stared at him a moment.

'Mr Hobby, you were loaned me by Mr DeTinc. Why don't you act just as if you were working over at the studio? I'll be through in another half-hour.'

'What do I get out of it?' he demanded, 'I'm no poser – I'm a writer.'

'Your studio salary has not stopped,' she said, resuming her work. 'What does it matter if Mr DeTinc wants you to do this?'

'It's different. You're a dame. I've got my self-respect to think of.'

'What do you expect me to do – flirt with you?'

'No – that's old stuff. But I thought we could sit around and have a drink.'

'Perhaps later,' she said, and then 'Is this harder work than the studio? Am I so difficult to look at?'

'I don't mind looking at you but why couldn't we sit on the sofa?'

'You don't sit on the sofa at the studio.'

'Sure you do. Listen, if you tried all the doors in the Writers' Building you'd find a lot of them locked and don't you forget it.'

She stepped back and squinted at him.

'Locked? To be undisturbed?' She put down her brush. 'I'll get you a drink.'

When she returned she stopped for a moment in the doorway – Pat had removed his shirt and stood rather sheepishly in the middle of the floor holding it toward her.

'Here's that shirt,' he said. 'You can have it. I know where I can get a lot more.'

For a moment longer she regarded him; then she took the shirt and put it on the sofa.

'Sit down and let me finish,' she said. As he hesitated she added, 'Then we'll have a drink together.'

'When'll that be ?'

'Fifteen minutes.'

She worked quickly – several times she was content with the lower face – several times she deliberated and started over. Something that she had seen in the commissary was missing.

'Been an artist a long time ?' Pat asked.

'Many years.'

'Been around artists' studios a lot ?'

'Quite a lot – I've had my own studios.'

'I guess a lot goes on around those studios. Did you ever – '

He hesitated.

'Ever what ?' she queried.

'Did you ever paint a naked man ?'

'Don't talk for one minute, please.' She paused with brush uplifted, seemed to listen, then made a swift stroke and looked doubtfully at the result.

'Do you know you're difficult to paint ?' she said, laying down the brush.

'I don't like this posing around,' he admitted. 'Let's call it a day.' He stood up. 'Why don't you – why don't you slip into something so you'll be comfortable ?'

The Princess smiled. She would tell her friends this story – it would sort of go with the picture, if the picture was any good, which she now doubted.

'You ought to revise your methods,' she said. 'Do you have much success with this approach ?'

Pat lit a cigarette and sat down.

'If you were eighteen, see, I'd give you that line about being nuts about you.'

'But why any line at all ?'

'Oh, come off it!' he advised her. 'You wanted to paint me, didn't you?'

'Yes.'

'Well, when a dame wants to paint a guy – ' Pat reached down and undid his shoe strings, kicked his shoes onto the floor, put his stockinged feet on the couch. ' – when a dame wants to see a guy about something or a guy wants to see a dame, there's a payoff, see.'

The Princess sighed. 'Well I seem to be trapped,' she said. 'But it makes it rather difficult when a dame just wants to paint a guy.'

'When a dame wants to paint a guy – ' Pat half closed his eyes, nodded and flapped his hands expressively. As his thumbs went suddenly toward his suspenders, she spoke in a louder voice.

'Officer!'

There was a sound behind Pat. He turned to see a young man in khaki with shining black gloves, standing in the door.

'Officer, this man is an employee of Mr DeTinc's. Mr DeTinc lent him to me for the afternoon.'

The policeman looked at the staring image of guilt upon the couch.

'Get fresh?' he inquired.

'I don't want to prefer charges – I called the desk to be on the safe side. He was to pose for me in the nude and now he refuses.' She walked casually to her easel. 'Mr Hobby, why don't you stop this mock-modesty – you'll find a turkish towel in the bathroom.'

Pat reached stupidly for his shoes. Somehow it flashed into his mind that they were running the eighth race at Santa Anita –

'Shake it up, you,' said the cop. 'You heard what the lady said.'

Pat stood up vaguely and fixed a long poignant look on the Princess.

'You told me – ' he said hoarsely, 'you wanted to paint –'

'You told me I meant something else. Hurry please. And officer, there's a drink in the pantry.'

... A few minutes later as Pat sat shivering in the center of the room his memory went back to those peep-shows of his youth – though at the moment he could see little resemblance. He was grateful at least for the turkish towel, even now failing to realize that the Princess was not interested in his shattered frame but in his face.

It wore the exact expression that had wooed her in the commissary, the expression of Hollywood and Vine, the other self of Mr DeTinc – and she worked fast while there was still light enough to paint by.

Two Old-Timers

Phil Macedon, once the Star of Stars, and Pat Hobby, script writer, had collided out on Sunset near the Beverly Hills Hotel. It was five in the morning and there was liquor in the air as they argued and Sergeant Gaspar took them around to the station house. Pat Hobby, a man of forty-nine, showed fight, apparently because Phil Macedon failed to acknowledge that they were old acquaintances.

He accidentally bumped Sergeant Gaspar who was so provoked that he put him in a little barred room while they waited for the Captain to arrive.

Chronologically Phil Macedon belonged between Eugene O'Brien and Robert Taylor. He was still a handsome man in his early fifties and he had saved enough from his great days for a hacienda in the San Fernando Valley; there he rested as full of honors, as rolicksome and with the same purposes in life as Man o' War.

With Pat Hobby life had dealt otherwise. After twenty-one years in the industry, script and publicity, the accident found him driving a 1933 car which had lately become the property of the North Hollywood Finance and Loan Co. And once, back in 1928, he had reached a point of getting bids for a private swimming pool.

He glowered from his confinement, still resenting Macedon's failure to acknowledge that they had ever met before.

'I suppose you don't remember Coleman,' he said sarcastically. 'Or Connie Talmadge or Bill Corker or Allan Dwan.'

Macedon lit a cigarette with the sort of timing in which the silent screen has never been surpassed, and offered one to Sergeant Gaspar.

'Couldn't I come in tomorrow ?' he asked. 'I have a horse to exercise – '

'I'm sorry, Mr Macedon,' said the cop – sincerely for the actor was an old favorite of his. 'The Captain is due here any minute. After that we won't be holding *you*.'

'It's just a formality,' said Pat, from his cell.

'Yeah, it's just a – ' Sergeant Gaspar glared at Pat. 'It may not be any formality for *you*. Did you ever hear of the sobriety test ?'

Macedon flicked his cigarette out the door and lit another.

'Suppose I come back in a couple of hours,' he suggested.

'No,' regretted Sergeant Gaspar. 'And since I have to detain you, Mr Macedon, I want to take the opportunity to tell you what you meant to me once. It was that picture you made, *The Final Push*, it meant a lot to every man who was in the war.'

'Oh, yes,' said Macedon, smiling.

'I used to try to tell my wife about the war – how it was, with the shells and the machine guns – I was in there seven months with the 26th New England – but she never understood. She'd point her finger at me and say "Boom! you're dead," and so I'd laugh and stop trying to make her understand.'

'Hey, can I get out of here ?' demanded Pat.

'You shut up!' said Gaspar fiercely. 'You probably wasn't in the war.'

'I was in the Motion Picture Home Guard,' said Pat. 'I had bad eyes.'

'Listen to him,' said Gaspar disgustedly. 'That's what all

them slackers say. Well, the war was *some*thing. And after my wife saw that picture of yours I never had to explain to her. She knew. She always spoke different about it after that – never just pointed her finger at me and said "Boom!" I'll never forget the part where you was in that shell hole. That was so real it made my hands sweat.'

'Thanks,' said Macedon graciously. He lit another cigarette, 'You see, I was in the war myself and I knew how it was. I knew how it felt.'

'Yes sir,' said Gaspar appreciatively. 'Well, I'm glad of the opportunity to tell you what you did for me. You – you explained the war to my wife.'

'What are you talking about?' demanded Pat Hobby suddenly. 'That war picture Bill Corker did in 1925?'

'There he goes again,' said Gaspar. 'Sure – *The Birth of a Nation*. Now you pipe down till the Captain comes.'

'Phil Macedon knew me then all right,' said Pat resentfully, 'I even watched him work on it one day.'

'I just don't happen to remember you, old man,' said Macedon politely, 'I can't help that.'

'You remember the day Bill Corker shot that shell hole sequence don't you? Your first day on the picture?'

There was a moment's silence.

'When will the Captain be here?' Macedon asked.

'Any minute now,' Mr Macedon.'

'Well, I remember,' said Pat, ' – because I was there when he had that shell hole dug. He was out there on the back lot at nine o'clock in the morning with a gang of hunkies to dig the hole and four cameras. He called you up from a field telephone and told you to go to the costumer and get into a soldier suit. Now you remember?'

'I don't load my mind with details, old man.'

'You called up that they didn't have one to fit you and

Corker told you to shut up and get into one anyhow. When you got out to the back lot you were sore as hell because your suit didn't fit.'

Macedon smiled charmingly.

'You have a most remarkable memory. Are you sure you have the right picture – and the right actor?' he asked.

'Am I!' said Pat grimly. 'I can see you right now. Only you didn't have much time to complain about the uniform because that wasn't Corker's plan. He always thought you were the toughest ham in Hollywood to get anything natural out of – and he had a scheme. He was going to get the heart of the picture shot by noon – before you even knew you were acting. He turned you around and shoved you down into that shell hole on your fanny, and yelled "Camera".'

'That's a lie,' said Phil Macedon. 'I *got* down.'

'Then why did you start yelling?' demanded Pat. 'I can still hear you: "Hey, what's the idea! Is this some — — gag? You get me out of here or I'll walk out on you!"

' – and all the time you were trying to claw your way up the side of that pit, so damn mad you couldn't see. You'd almost get up and then you'd slide back and lie there with your face working – till finally you began to bawl and all this time Bill had four cameras on you. After about twenty minutes you gave up and just lay there, heaving. Bill took a hundred feet of that and then he had a couple of prop men pull you out.'

The police Captain had arrived in the squad car. He stood in the doorway against the first grey of dawn.

'What you got here, Sergeant? A drunk?'

Sergeant Gaspar walked over to the cell, unlocked it and beckoned Pat to come out. Pat blinked a moment – then his eyes fell on Phil Macedon and he shook his finger at him.

'So you see I *do* know you,' he said. 'Bill Corker cut that piece of film and titled it so you were supposed to be a doughboy whose pal had just been killed. You wanted to climb out and get at the Germans in revenge, but the shells bursting all around and the concussions kept knocking you back in.'

'What's it about?' demanded the Captain.

'I want to prove I know this guy,' said Pat. 'Bill said the best moment in the picture was when Phil was yelling "I've al*ready* broken my first finger nail!" Bill titled it "Ten Huns will go to hell to shine your shoes!" '

'You've got here "collision with alcohol",' said the Captain looking at the blotter. 'Let's take these guys down to the hospital and give them the test.'

'Look here now,' said the actor, with his flashing smile, 'my name's Phil Macedon.'

The Captain was a political appointee and very young. He remembered the name and the face but he was not especially impressed because Hollywood was full of has-beens.

They all got into the squad car at the door.

After the test Macedon was held at the station house until friends could arrange bail. Pat Hobby was discharged but his car would not run, so Sergeant Gaspar offered to drive him home.

'Where do you live?' he asked as they started off.

'I don't live anywhere tonight,' said Pat. 'That's why I was driving around. When a friend of mine wakes up I'll touch him for a couple of bucks and go to a hotel.'

'Well now,' said Sergeant Gaspar, 'I got a couple of bucks that ain't working.'

The great mansions of Beverly Hills slid by and Pat waved his hand at them in salute.

'In the good old days,' he said, 'I used to be able to drop

into some of those houses day or night. And Sunday morn-
ings – '

'Is that all true you said in the station,' Gaspar asked,
' – about how they put him in the hole ?'

'Sure, it is,' said Pat. 'That guy needn't have been so up-
stage. He's just an old-timer like me.'

Mightier Than the Sword

The swarthy man, with eyes that snapped back and forward on a rubber band from the rear of his head, answered to the alias of Dick Dale. The tall, spectacled man who was put together like a camel without a hump – and you missed the hump – answered to the name of E. Brunswick Hudson. The scene was a shoeshine stand, insignificant unit of the great studio. We perceive it through the red-rimmed eyes of Pat Hobby who sat in the chair beside Director Dale.

The stand was out of doors, opposite the commissary. The voice of E. Brunswick Hudson quivered with passion but it was pitched low so as not to reach passers-by.

'I don't know what a writer like me is doing out here anyhow,' he said, with vibrations.

Pat Hobby, who was an old-timer, could have supplied the answer, but he had not the acquaintance of the other two.

'It's a funny business,' said Dick Dale, and to the shoeshine boy, 'Use that saddle soap.'

'Funny!' thundered E., 'It's suspect! Here against my better judgement I write just what you tell me – and the office tells me to get out because we can't seem to agree.'

'That's polite,' explained Dick Dale. 'What do you want me to do – knock you down ?'

E. Brunswick Hudson removed his glasses.

'Try it!' he suggested. 'I weigh a hundred and sixty-two and I haven't got an ounce of flesh on me.' He hesitated and redeemed himself from this extremity. 'I mean *fat* on me.'

'Oh, to hell with that!' said Dick Dale contemptuously, 'I can't mix it up with you. I got to figure this picture. You go back East and write one of your books and forget it.' Momentarily he looked at Pat Hobby, smiling as if *he* would understand, as if anyone would understand except E. Brunswick Hudson. 'I can't tell you all about pictures in three weeks.'

Hudson replaced his spectacles.

'When I *do* write a book,' he said, 'I'll make you the laughing stock of the nation.'

He withdrew, ineffectual, baffled, defeated. After a minute Pat spoke.

'Those guys can never get the idea,' he commented. 'I've never seen one get the idea and I been in this business, publicity and script, for twenty years.'

'You on the lot ?' Dale asked.

Pat hesitated.

'Just finished a job,' he said.

That was five months before.

'What screen credits you got ?' Dale asked.

'I got credits going all the way back to 1920.'

'Come up to my office,' Dick Dale said, 'I got something I'd like to talk over – now that bastard is gone back to his New England farm. Why do they have to get a New England farm – with the whole West not settled ?'

Pat gave his second-to-last dime to the bootblack and climbed down from the stand.

II

We are in the midst of technicalities.

'The trouble is this composer Reginald de Koven didn't have any color,' said Dick Dale. 'He wasn't deaf like

Beethoven or a singing waiter or get put in jail or anything. All he did was write music and all we got for an angle is that song *O Promise Me*. We got to weave something around that – a dame promises him something and in the end he collects.'

'I want time to think it over in my mind,' said Pat. 'If Jack Berners will put me on the picture – '

'He'll put you on,' said Dick Dale. 'From now on I'm picking my own writers. What do you get – fifteen hundred?' He looked at Pat's shoes. 'Seven-fifty?'

Pat stared at him blankly for a moment; then out of thin air, produced his best piece of imaginative fiction in a decade.

'I was mixed up with a producer's wife,' he said, 'and they ganged up on me. I only get three-fifty now.'

In some ways it was the easiest job he had ever had. Director Dick Dale was a type that, fifty years ago, could be found in any American town. Generally he was the local photographer, usually he was the originator of small mechanical contrivances and a leader in bizarre local movements, almost always he contributed verse to the local press. All the most energetic embodiments of this 'Sensation Type' had migrated to Hollywood between 1910 and 1930, and there they had achieved a psychological fulfilment inconceivable in any other time or place. At last, and on a large scale, they were able to have their way. In the weeks that Pat Hobby and Mabel Hatman, Mr Dale's script girl, sat beside him and worked on the script, not a movement, not a word went into it that was not Dick Dale's coinage. Pat would venture a suggestion, something that was 'Always good'.

'Wait a minute! Wait a minute!' Dick Dale was on his feet, his hands outspread. 'I seem to see a dog.' They would wait, tense and breathless, while he saw a dog.

'Two dogs.'

A second dog took its place beside the first in their obedient visions.

'We open on a dog on a leash – pull the camera back to show another dog – now they're snapping at each other. We pull back further – the leashes are attached to tables – the tables tip over. See it?'

Or else, out of a clear sky.

'I seem to see De Koven as a plasterer's apprentice.'

'Yes.' This hopefully.

'He goes to Santa Anita and plasters the walls, singing at his work. Take that down, Mabel.' He continued on ...

In a month they had the requisite hundred and twenty pages. Reginald de Koven, it seemed, though not an alcoholic, was too fond of 'The Little Brown Jug'. The father of the girl he loved had died of drink, and after the wedding when she found him drinking from the Little Brown Jug, nothing would do but that she should go away, for twenty years. He became famous and she sang his songs as Maid Marian but he never knew it was the same girl.

The script, marked 'Temporary Complete. From Pat Hobby' went up to the head office. The schedule called for Dale to begin shooting in a week.

Twenty-four hours later he sat with his staff in his office, in an atmosphere of blue gloom. Pat Hobby was the least depressed. Four weeks at three-fifty, even allowing for the two hundred that had slipped away at Santa Anita, was a far cry from the twenty cents he had owned on the shoe-shine stand.

'That's pictures, Dick,' he said consolingly. 'You're up – you're down – you're in, you're out. Any old-timer knows.'

'Yes,' said Dick Dale absently. 'Mabel, phone that E.

Brunswick Hudson. He's on his New England farm – maybe milking bees.'

In a few minutes she reported.

'He flew into Hollywood this morning, Mr Dale. I've located him at the Beverly Wilshire Hotel.'

Dick Dale pressed his ear to the phone. His voice was bland and friendly as he said:

'Mr Hudson, there was one day here you had an idea I liked. You said you were going to write it up. It was about this De Koven stealing his music from a sheepherder up in Vermont. Remember ?'

'Yes.'

'Well, Berners wants to go into production right away, or else we can't have the cast, so we're on the spot, if you know what I mean. Do you happen to have that stuff ?'

'You remember when I brought it to you ?' Hudson asked. 'You kept me waiting two hours – then you looked at it for two minutes. Your neck hurt you – I think it needed wringing. God, how it hurt you. That was the only nice thing about that morning.'

'In picture business – '

'I'm so glad you're stuck. I wouldn't tell you the story of *The Three Bears* for fifty grand.'

As the phones clicked Dick Dale turned to Pat.

'Goddam writers!' he said savagely. 'What do we pay you for ? Millions – and you write a lot of tripe I can't photograph and get sore if we don't read your lousy stuff! How can a man make pictures when they give me two bastards like you and Hudson. How ? How do you think – you old whiskey bum!'

Pat rose – took a step toward the door. He didn't know, he said.

'Get out of here!' cried Dick Dale. 'You're off the payroll. Get off the lot.'

Fate had not dealt Pat a farm in New England, but there was a café just across from the studio where bucolic dreams blossomed in bottles if you had the money. He did not like to leave the lot, which for many years had been home for him, so he came back at six and went up to his office. It was locked. He saw that they had already allotted it to another writer – the name on the door was E. Brunswick Hudson.

He spent an hour in the commissary, made another visit to the bar, and then some instinct led him to a stage where there was a bedroom set. He passed the night upon a couch occupied by Claudette Colbert in the fluffiest ruffles only that afternoon.

Morning was bleaker, but he had a little in his bottle and almost a hundred dollars in his pocket. The horses were running at Santa Anita and he might double it by night.

On his way out of the lot he hesitated beside the barber shop but he felt too nervous for a shave. Then he paused, for from the direction of the shoeshine stand he heard Dick Dale's voice.

'Miss Hatman found your other script, and it happens to be the property of the company.'

E. Brunswick Hudson stood at the foot of the stand.

'I won't have my name used,' he said.

'That's good. I'll put her name on it. Berners thinks it's great, if the De Koven family will stand for it. Hell – the sheepbreeder never would have been able to market those tunes anyhow. Ever hear of any sheepherder drawing down jack from ASCAP?'

Hudson took off his spectacles.

'I weigh a hundred and sixty-three – '

Pat moved in closer.

'Join the army,' said Dale contemptuously, 'I got no time

for mixing it up. I got to make a picture.' His eyes fell on Pat. 'Hello old-timer.'

'Hello Dick,' said Pat smiling. Then knowing the advantage of the psychological moment he took his chance.

'When do we work ?' he said.

'How much ?' Dick Dale asked the shoeshine boy – and to Pat, 'It's all done. I promised Mabel a screen credit for a long time. Look me up some day when you got an idea.'

He hailed someone by the barber shop and hurried off. Hudson and Hobby, men of letters who had never met, regarded each other. There were tears of anger in Hudson's eyes.

'Authors get a tough break out here,' Pat said sympathetically. 'They never ought to come.'

'Who'd make up the stories – these feebs ?'

'Well anyhow, not authors,' said Pat. 'They don't want authors. They want writers – like me.'

Pat Hobby's College Days

The afternoon was dark. The walls of Topanga Canyon rose sheer on either side. Get rid of it she must. The clank clank in the back seat frightened her. Evylyn did not like the business at all. It was not what she came out here to do. Then she thought of Mr Hobby. He believed in her, trusted her – and she was doing this for him.

But the mission was arduous. Evylyn Lascalles left the canyon and cruised along the inhospitable shores of Beverly Hills. Several times she turned up alleys, several times she parked beside vacant lots – but always some pedestrian or loiterer threw her into a mood of nervous anxiety. Once her heart almost stopped as she was eyed with appreciation – or was it suspicion – by a man who looked like a detective.

– He had no right to ask me this, she said to herself. Never again. I'll tell him so. Never again.

Night was fast descending. Evylyn Lascalles had never seen it come down so fast. Back to the canyon then, to the wild, free life. She drove up a paint-box corridor which gave its last pastel shades to the day. And reached a certain security at a bend overlooking plateau land far below.

Here there could be no complication. As she threw each article over the cliff it would be as far removed from her as if she were in a different state of the Union.

Miss Lascalles was from Brooklyn. She had wanted very much to come to Hollywood and be a secretary in pictures – now she wished that she had never left her home.

On with the job though – she must part with her cargo – as soon as this next car passed the bend. . . .

II

. . . Meanwhile her employer, Pat Hobby, stood in front of the barber shop talking to Louie, the Studio Bookie. Pat's four weeks at two-fifty would be up tomorrow and he had begun to have that harassed and aghast feeling of those who live always on the edge of solvency.

'Four lousy weeks on a bad script,' he said. 'That's all I've had in six months.'

'How do you live?' asked Louie – without *too* much show of interest.

'I don't live. The days go by, the weeks go by. But who cares? Who cares – after twenty years.'

'You had a good time in your day,' Louie reminded him.

Pat looked after a dress extra in a shimmering lamé gown.

'Sure,' he admitted, 'I had three wives. All anybody could want.'

'You mean *that* was one of your wives?' asked Louie.

Pat peered after the disappearing figure.

'No-o. I didn't say *that* was one. But I've had plenty of them feeding out of my pocket. Not now though – a man of forty-nine is not considered human.'

'You've got a cute little secretary,' said Louie. 'Look Pat, I'll give you a tip –'

'Can't use it,' said Pat, 'I got fifty cents.'

'I don't mean that kind of tip. Listen – Jack Berners wants to make a picture about U.W.C. because he's got a kid there that plays basketball. He can't get a story. Why don't you go over and see the Athaletic Superintendent named Doolan at U.W.C.? That superintendent owes me three grand on the nags, and he could maybe give you an idea for a college picture. And then you bring it back and sell it to Berners. You're on salary, ain't you?'

'Till tomorrow,' said Pat gloomily.

'Go and see Jim Kresge that hangs out in the Campus Sport Shop. He'll introduce you to the Athaletic Superintendent. Look, Pat, I got to make a collection now. Just remember, Pat, that Doolan owes me three grand.'

III

It didn't seem hopeful to Pat but it was better than nothing. Returning for his coat to his room in the Writers' Building he was in time to pick up a plainting telephone.

'This is Evylyn,' said a fluttering voice. 'I can't get rid of it this afternoon. There's cars on every road –'

'I can't talk about it here,' said Pat quickly, 'I got to go over to U.W.C. on a notion.'

'I've tried,' she wailed, ' – and *tried*! And every time, some car comes along –'

'Aw, please!' He hung up – he had enough on his mind.

For years Pat had followed the deeds of 'the Trojums' of U.S.C. and the almost as fabulous doings of 'the Roller Coasters', who represented the Univ. of the Western Coast. His interest was not so much physiological, tactical or intellectual as it was mathematical – but the Rollers had cost him plenty in their day – and thus it was with a sense of vague proprietorship that he stepped upon the half De Mille, half Aztec campus.

He located Kresge who conducted him to Superintendent Kit Doolan. Mr Doolan, a famous ex-tackle, was in excellent humor. With five colored giants in this year's line, none of them quite old enough for pensions, but all men of experience, his team was in a fair way to conquer his section.

'Glad to be of help to your studio,' he said. 'Glad to help Mr Berners – or Louie. What can I do for you? You want to make a picture? ... Well, we can always use publicity. Mr Hobby, I got a meeting of the Faculty Committee in just five minutes and perhaps you'd like to tell them your notion.'

'I don't know,' said Pat doubtfully. 'What I thought was maybe I could have a spiel with you. We could go somewhere and hoist one.'

'Afraid not,' said Doolan jovially. 'If those smarties smelt liquor on me – Boy! Come on over to the meeting – somebody's been getting away with watches and jewelry on the campus and we're sure it's a student.'

Mr Kresge, having played his role, got up to leave.

'Like something good for the fifth tomorrow?'

'Not me,' said Mr Doolan.

'You, Mr Hobby?'

'Not me,' said Pat.

IV

Ending their alliance with the underworld, Pat Hobby and Superintendent Doolan walked down the corridor of the Administration Building. Outside the Dean's office Doolan said:

'As soon as I can, I'll bring you in and introduce you.'

As an accredited representative neither of Jack Berners' nor of the studio, Pat waited with a certain *malaise*. He did not look forward to confronting a group of highbrows but he remembered that he bore an humble but warming piece of merchandise in his threadbare overcoat. The Dean's assistant had left her desk to take notes at the conference so he repleated his calories with a long, gagging draught.

In a moment, there was a responsive glow and he settled

down in his chair, his eye fixed on the door marked:

SAMUEL K. WISKETH
DEAN OF THE STUDENT BODY

It might be a somewhat formidable encounter.

... but why? There were stuffed shirts – everybody knew that. They had college degrees but they could be bought. If they'd play ball with the studio they'd get a lot of good publicity for U.W.C. And that meant bigger salaries for them, didn't it, and more jack?

The door to the conference room opened and closed tentatively. No one came out but Pat sat up and readied himself. Representing the fourth biggest industry in America, or *al*most representing it, he must not let a bunch of highbrows stare him down. He was not without an inside view of higher education – in his early youth he had once been the 'Buttons' in the DKE House at the University of Pennsylvania. And with encouraging chauvinism he assured himself that Pennsylvania had it over this pioneer enterprise like a tent.

The door opened – a flustered young man with beads of sweat on his forehead came tearing out, tore through – and disappeared. Mr Doolan stood calmly in the doorway.

'All right, Mr Hobby,' he said.

Nothing to be scared of. Memories of old college days continued to flood over Pat as he walked in. And instantaneously, as the juice of confidence flowed through his system, he had his idea. . . .

'. . . it's more of a realistic idea,' he was saying five minutes later 'Understand?'

Dean Wiskith, a tall, pale man with an earphone, seemed to understand – if not exactly to approve. Pat hammered in his point again.

'It's up-to-the-minute,' he said patiently, 'what we call "a topical". You admit that young squirt who went out of here was stealing watches, don't you?'

The faculty committee, all except Doolan, exchanged glances, but no one interrupted.

'There you are,' went on Pat triumphantly. 'You turn him in to the newspapers. But here's the twist. In the Picture we make it turns out he steals the watches to support his young *brother* – and his young brother is the mainstay of the football team! He's the climax runner. We probably try to borrow Tyrone Power but we use one of *your* players as a double.'

Pat paused, trying to think of everything.

' – of course, we've got to release it in the southern states, so it's got to be one of your players that's white.'

There was an unquiet pause. Mr Doolan came to his rescue.

'Not a bad idea,' he suggested.

'It's an appalling idea,' broke out Dean Wiskith. 'It's – '

Doolan's face tightened slowly.

'Wait a minute,' he said. 'Who's telling *who* around here? You listen to *him*!'

The Dean's assistant, who had recently vanished from the room at the call of a buzzer, had reappeared and was whispering in the Dean's ear. The latter started.

'Just a minute, Mr Doolan,' he said. He turned to the other members of the committee.

'The proctor has a disciplinary case outside and he can't legally hold the offender. Can we settle it first? And then get back to this – ' He glared at Mr Doolan, ' – to this pre*post*erous idea?'

At his nod the assistant opened the door.

This proctor, thought Pat, ranging back to his days on

the vineclad, leafy campus, looked like all proctors, an intimidated cop, a scarcely civilized beast of prey.

'Gentlemen,' the proctor said, with delicately modulated respect, 'I've got something that can't be explained away.' He shook his head, puzzled, and then continued: 'I know it's all wrong – but *I* can't seem to get to the point of it. I'd like to turn it over to *you* – I'll just show you the evidence and the offender . . . Come in, you.'

As Evylyn Lascalles entered, followed shortly by a big clinking pillow cover which the proctor deposited beside her, Pat thought once more of the elm-covered campus of the University of Pennsylvania. He wished passionately that he were there. He wished it more than anything in the world. Next to that he wished that Doolan's back, behind which he tried to hide by a shifting of his chair, were broader still.

'There you are!' she cried gratefully. 'Oh, Mr Hobby – Thank God! I couldn't get rid of them – and I couldn't take them home – my mother would kill me. So I came here to find you – and this man packed into the back seat of my car.'

'What's in that sack?' demanded Dean Wiskith, 'Bombs? What?'

Seconds before the proctor had picked up the sack and bounced it on the floor, so that it gave out a clear unmistakable sound, Pat could have told them. There were dead soldiers – pints, half-pints, quarts – the evidence of four strained weeks at two-fifty – empty bottles collected from his office drawers. Since his contract was up tomorrow he had thought it best not to leave such witnesses behind.

Seeking for escape his mind reached back for the last time to those careless days of fetch and carry at the University of Pennsylvania.

'I'll take it,' he said rising.

Slinging the sack over his shoulder, he faced the faculty committee and said surprisingly:

'Think it over.'

v

'We did,' Mr Doolan told his wife that night. 'But we never made head nor tail of it.'

'It's kind of spooky,' said Mrs Doolan. 'I hope I don't dream tonight. The poor man with that sack! I keep thinking he'll be down in purgatory – and they'll make him carve a ship in *every one* of those bottles -- before he can go to heaven.'

'Don't!' said Doolan quickly. 'You'll have *me* dreaming. There were plenty bottles.'

Appendix

The following is the revision of *A Patriotic Short*, received October 15 1940, too late to incorporate its changes into the version that was then on press for the December 1940 issue of *Esquire*, which, though dated December, actually appeared on November 15. Double underlining indicates changes or additions, while the slant (/) calls the reader's attention to those places where material was either excised or transposed elsewhere in the story.

A PATRIOTIC SHORT

by

F. SCOTT FITZGERALD

Pat Hobby, the Writer and the Man, had his great
success in Hollywood in an era described by Irving Cobb
as /"when you had to have a shin-bone of St. Sebastian for
a clutch lever." /You had to have a pool too and Pat had
one--at least he had one for the first few hours after it
was filled every week, before it stubbornly seeped away
through the cracks in the cement.

"But it was a pool," he assured himself one afternoon
more than ten years later. /Now he was more than grateful
for a small chore/at two-fifty a week/but all the years
of failure could not take the beautiful memory away.

/He was working on an humble "short." It was pre-
cariously based on the career of General Fitzhugh Lee who
fought for the Confederacy and later for the U.S./against
Spain--so it would offend neither North nor South. /In/
conference Pat had tried to cooperate.

"I was thinking--" he suggested to Jack Berners,
"--that it might be a good thing nowadays if we could give
it a Jewish touch."

"What do you mean?" demanded Jack Berners quickly. .

"Well I thought--the way things are and all, it would be a sort of good thing to show that there were /Jews in it too."

"In what?"

"In the Civil War." Quickly Pat reviewed his meager history. "They were, weren't they?"

"I suppose so," said Berners, with some impatience, "I suppose everybody was in it--except /Quakers."

"Well, my idea was that we could have this Fitzhugh Lee in love with a Jewish girl. He's going to be shot at curfew so she grabs the church bell--"

Jack Berners leaned forward earnestly.

"Say, Pat, you want this job, don't you?"

"Sure, I do."

"Well, I told you the story we want. / The Jews can take care of themselves, and if you thought up this tripe to please me you're losing your grip."

Was that a way to treat a man who had once owned a pool? / The reason Pat kept thinking about his long lost pool was because of the President of the United States. Pat was remembering a certain day, a decade ago, in every detail. / On that day word had gone around that the President was going to visit the lot. It seemed to mark a new era in pictures because the President of the United States had never visited a studio before. The executives of the company were all dressed up with ties and there were flags over the commissary door...

The voice of Ben Brown, the head of the shorts
department.broke in on Pat's reverie.

"Jack Berners just phoned me," he said, "We don't
want any new angles, Pat. We got a history. Fitzhugh Lee
was in the cavalry. He was a nephew of Robert E. Lee and
we want to show him surrendering at Appomax, pretty sore
and all that. And then show how he got reconciled--
we'll have to be careful because Virginia is still lousy
with Lees--and how he finally accepts a U.S. commission
from McKinley. And clean up the stuff about Spain--the
guy that wrote it was a Red and he's got all the Spanish
officers having ants in their pants."

In his office Pat looked at the script of "True to
Two Flags." The first scene showed General Fitzhugh Lee
at the head of his cavalry receiving word that Petersburg
had been evacuated. In the script Lee took the blow in
lively pantomime, but Pat was getting two-fifty a week--
so, casually and without effort, he wrote in one of his
favorite lines of dialogue.

> LEE (To his officers).
>
> Well, what are you standing here
> gawking for? Do something!

6. MEDIUM SHOT. OFFICERS - pepping up, slapping each
other on back etc.

> Dissolve to:

Dissolve to what? Pat's mind dissolved once more
into the glamorous past. On that great day ten years before

his phone in his office had rung at noon. It was Mr. Moskin.

"Pat, the President is lunching in the Executives'
Dining Room. Doug Fairbanks can't come so there's a place
empty and anyhow we think there ought to be one writer there."

His memory of the luncheon was palpitant with glamor.
The great man had asked questions about pictures and told a
joke, and Pat had laughed uproariously with the others--all
of them solid men together--rich, happy, successful.

Afterwards the President was to see some scenes
taken on a set, and still later he was going to Mr. Moskin's
house to meet several women stars at tea. Pat was not
invited to that party, but his Beverly Hills home was next
door to Mr. Moskin's mansion and he went home early. From
his veranda he saw the cortège drive up, with Mr. Moskin
beside the President in the back seat. He was proud of
pictures then--of the position he had won in them--of the
President of the happy country where pictures were born...

Pat sighed. Returning once more to reality he looked
down at the script of "True to Two Flags" and wrote
slowly and thoughtfully:
INSERT: A CALENDAR -- with the years plainly marked and
the sheets blowing off in a cold wind, to indicate that
Fitzhugh Lee is growing older and older.

Pat's labors had made him thirsty--not for water,
but he knew better than to take anything else his first day
on the job. He went out into the hall and along the
corridor to the cooler--and as he walked he slipped back
into his reverie of things past...

It had been a lovely California afternoon so
Mr. Moskin had taken his exalted guest and the coterie of
stars into his garden, adjoining Pat's garden. Pat went
out his back door and followed a low privet hedge keeping
out of sight--and then accidentally came face to face
with the Presidential party.

The President smiled and nodded. Mr. Moskin smiled
and nodded.

"You met Mr. Hobby at lunch," Mr. Moskin said to
the President. "He's one of our writers."

"Oh yes," said the President, "You write the pictures?"

"Yes I do," said Pat.

The President glanced over into Pat's property.

"I suppose--" he said, "--that you get lots of
inspiration sitting by the side of that fine pool."

"Yes," said Pat, "Yes, I do."

...Pat filled his cup at the cooler/in the hall.
Down the hall there was a group approaching--Jack Berners,
Ben Brown and several other executives and with them a
girl to whom they were very attentive and deferential. He
recognized her face--she was the girl of the year, the
It Girl, the Oomph Girl, the Glamor Girl, the girl for
whose services every studio was in heavy competition.

Pat lingered over his drink. He had seen many
phonies break in and break out again, but this girl/was
someone to stir every pulse in the nation. His heart beat
faster--as the procession drew near, he put down the cup,
dabbed at his hair with his hand and took a step/into
the corridor.

The girl looked at him--he looked at the girl. Then
she took one arm of Jack Berners' and one of Ben Brown's
and, without the suggestion of an introduction, the party
walked right through him--so that he had to take a
step back against the wall.

An instant later Jack Berners turned around and
called back, "Hello, Pat." And one of the others glanced
around but no one else spoke, so interested were they
in the girl.

In his office Pat looked gloomily at the scene where
President McKinley offers a United States commission to
Fitzhugh Lee. Berners had written on the margin "Have
McKinley plug democracy and Cuban-American friendship--but
no cracks at Spain as market may improve." Pat gritted
his teeth and bore down on his pencil as he wrote:

LEE

Mr. President, you can take your

commission and go straight to Hell.

Then Pat bent down over his desk, his shoulders shaking
miserably as he thought of that happy day when he had
owned a swimming pool.

* * * *